Demon of the
Darkness

Demon of the Darkness

Dana Ross

Five Star
Unity, Maine

Five Star Romance Series.
Published in 2000 in conjunction with Maureen Moran
Agency.

Cover photograph © Alan J. La Vallee

Set in 11 pt. Plantin.

Printed in the United States on permanent paper.

Library of Congress Cataloging-in-Publication Data

Ross, Dana, 1912–
    Demon of the darkness / by Dana Ross.
      p. cm.
    ISBN 0-7862-2507-6 (hc : alk. paper)
    I. Title.
  PR9199.3.R5996 D42   2000
    813′.54—dc21
                                            00-023529

To Helen Emerson
— Faye's mother!

Chapter One

In looking back Susan Ward decided that the start of her dark suspicions of her handsome doctor husband had begun after his disappearance from their hotel room on that first night in London in 1889. They had arrived on shipboard from America and had decided to remain at the Grand Hotel for a few nights to cap their honeymoon. Following this they'd planned to move to her husband's house in a fashionable street near Marble Arch.

On the night in question she'd suddenly wakened to find that she was alone in bed. She'd raised herself on an elbow and stared into the darkness of the big room looking for some sign of her husband. But the room appeared to be as empty as the place in the bed beside her. She waited for a little and when there was no sign of him she got out of bed and made a careful search of their suite. He was not to be found and the clothes he'd placed carefully on the rack beside their bed were also gone. It was apparent that he had left the room to go out into the night somewhere fully dressed!

Susan had been startled and concerned. She'd gone to the nearest window and pulled aside the heavy drape to stare out into the street. The heavy fog which had greeted them on their arrival in London still lay over the old city like a gray cloak. Below at the street corner a gas lamp offered a faint glow of yellow to barely pierce the thick mist. It was long after midnight and the streets seemed empty as she stood there worrying where her husband might be and why he had left her without any explanation.

Allowing the drape to fall closed she moved across the dark room to the side of the bed and debated what she should do. To ring for service and inquire about her missing husband would probably not produce any result and might cause some scandal.

She stood there hesitantly, trying to decide where Terence might have gone and why. Her first thought was that someone in the hotel might have been taken ill and her doctor husband had been called on in the emergency. She was a fairly heavy sleeper and might have missed a knock on the door, his answering it and later dressing and leaving. The more she thought about it the more likely it appeared to be.

Having arrived at this decision she returned to bed. But she did not sleep. She was much too tense for that. Staring up into the shadows she listened for her husband to return. Every sound of the night came to her clearly. The dry rattle of carriage wheels in the street below, the eerie, frenzied scream of some denizen of the fog-ridden night, the quick passing of footsteps in the carpeted corridor outside the door of her suite. Probably the night valet returning shoes left to be polished at the various room doors.

And as she lay there caught between sleep and being fully awake she began to hazily review the events of the past several months which had brought her to this London hotel suite as the bride of British surgeon Dr. Terence Ward. It had all begun at a formal ball at the Beacon Street home of a Boston girl friend, Dorothea Sedgewick.

She and Dorothea had been the closest of friends at the Cambridge boarding school for young ladies which they'd both attended. It might have been called a school for wealthy young ladies since only the daughters of the rich were enrolled. Susan's home was in Philadelphia. Orphaned at an early age she had been brought up by her uncle Charles. Her parents had left her a considerable amount of money and her lawyer uncle was also wealthy.

Dorothea Sedgewick was also the daughter of socially elect, rich parents. They kept in touch with each other long after they attended the boarding school together, and so at Christmas, 1888, Dorothea invited her to come as her house guest and attend the grand formal ball her parents were giving on New Year's Eve to celebrate the advent of the coming year. Because life at home with her uncle Charles was very quiet Susan was delighted to accept the invitation.

The journey from Philadelphia to Boston by train in midwinter had been exciting. And when she'd arrived in the city she'd found it recovering from a fierce blizzard. Great mounds of snow still lined the streets with only room for a single sleigh to travel in places and some of the sidewalks had not been cleared at all.

But in spite of the snow and cold she was glad to be there with her friend. As they drove along in a sleigh up Beacon Street to the home of the Sedgewicks she admired the great red-brick and stone mansions with their façades draped with snow and icicles. The two big chestnuts drawing the sleigh made the bells on their harness jingle in a delightful fashion and the top-hatted driver seated at the front of the sleigh wore a heavy muffler and coat as protection against the cold. The two girls had a great black bear rug wrapped around them to keep them warm on the sunny December afternoon.

"I'm so glad you're here for the party," the blond and rather plain Dorothea bubbled. "I have the most wonderful man for you to meet!"

Susan's pert oval face framed by a red bonnet which covered most of her rather curly brown hair, showed a smile. Since Dorothea had become engaged to the son of a prominent Boston businessman the blond girl had turned into an inveterate matchmaker. It amused Susan.

"Who is it this time?" she'd asked.

"Someone you've never met before," Dorothea said with a teasing gleam in her blue eyes.

"I know that. But who?"

"An Englishman with divine manners . . . and he looks like Lord Byron! The same classical handsomeness and brooding manner, not to mention his dark hair."

"I've only met a few Englishmen," Susan had said. "And they have mostly been lawyer friends of my uncle. I found them rather dull."

"You won't find Dr. Terence Ward dull!" Dorothea had promised.

Her eyebrows lifted. "A doctor?"

"And young, middle-aged," her friend declared with this rather confusing description. "I mean he's young enough to be interesting to someone our age and yet old enough to be a doctor."

Susan's large brown eyes had mirrored her amusement at her friend's attempted description of this paragon of manhood. She asked, "And pray what is he doing in Boston?"

"He came over for a few months of special study and he's soon going to return. I've been hoping you'd get here in time to meet him."

Susan's pert face was smiling. "I assume this Dr. Terence Ward is a bachelor."

"No. A widower," her friend volunteered. "I have never heard the whole story. He intensely hates to discuss his wife's death. He must have loved her a great deal, I'd say. But I gather that her death was sudden and a shock to him."

"She must have died young," Susan said. "Have you any idea when it happened?"

"I'm not sure," Dorothea told her. "But I don't think it

was all that long ago. Maybe last year."

"How awful for him!" she said sympathetically.

"I agree. He's so nice and mostly sad," Dorothea said. "He needs another wife."

Susan laughed. "Don't glance at me in that fashion. I'm perfectly happy as housekeeper for my uncle."

Dorothea protested. "It's no life for you. First thing you know, you'll wind up an old maid!"

"What a dreadful thought!" she said, making a face and causing her friend to laugh as they drew up before the fine old three-story mansion on Beacon Street.

Actually the plight of being an old maid was not a pleasant one even if, like Susan, you possessed a lot of money. She had already seen most of her friends married, some even had two or three children, and now Dorothea was soon to be a bride. Susan knew that it was time she encountered a desirable man. Women who reached thirty were marked down as likely spinsters in the society she knew. At twenty-two she still had quite a few years' grace, but many of her friends had been married at eighteen and nineteen. By them she was even now regarded as an old maid.

Not that she was hopeful of Dorothea's matchmaking. Her friends' efforts in this line had been dismal failures before. Susan owed Dorothea for a nuisance courtship with a skinny, yellow-haired youth with bad breath and a weakness for gambling. Her uncle Charles had soon found out the condition of the young man's finances and sent him on his way. There had also been a young man of fine Boston family who'd ended every night in a drunken daze. She'd let him go!

So she hadn't been too optimistic about this new young man whom Dorothea had chosen for her. But she was told she'd meet him at the ball that was being given on New Year's Eve. Before that she had a glorious week of shopping in the

Boston stores, skating in the Public Garden, having afternoon tea with old friends, and sleighing as far as Cambridge.

Then came the day of the gala event. The day had been cold and she and Dorothea had mostly spent it indoors watching the servants decorate the big ballroom with greenery, bright ornaments, and colorful ribbons. A platform was installed for the orchestra in one corner of the large room and a long white-clothed table was set out in another for the punch bowl and other liquors which would be served the guests.

"Right after midnight there is to be a fine supper served in the dining room," Dorothea told her. "Cook is getting things ready for it now. In fact, she's been preparing for it all week."

"How many guests will there be?" she'd asked.

"About fifty," Dorothea said. And with a knowing smile, she added, "Dr. Terence Ward will be among them!"

The next big excitement had been dressing for the party. She and Dorothea had journeyed back and forth from room to room, checking on each other's progress, until the maids in attendance were in despair of ever getting them ready. Dorothea had a new gown of red organdy and Susan had chosen a soft shade of green taffeta. By the time they were dressed the orchestra was already playing.

Guests were beginning to arrive, and Dorothea's young man at once whisked her off for a lively waltz. Susan watched from the sidelines, impressed by the lovely gowns of the women of all ages and their escorts attired in white tie and tails. It was an exciting party.

One of the older gentleman guests, a stout sexagenarian with gray side-whiskers, came and bowed to her. "They are about to play a mazurka, my dear, may I have the pleasure?"

"I'm only a modest dancer," she warned him.

Leading her out by the hand with a pleased expression on

his florid face the old man said, "What you may lack in grace you more than make up for in beauty!"

They took their places as the violinist leading the orchestra gave the signal to begin. The music was excellent and so was her partner. Susan quickly lost herself in the excitement of the dance. The big room with its gas-lit chandeliers and gay, seasonal decorations seemed to whirl around her as she went through the steps of the lively mazurka.

When it finally ended her partner was short of breath and perspiring. But as he led her off the floor, he said, "You are a fine dancer, young lady."

She saw that Dorothea was waiting for her so she thanked the old gentleman and went across to join her friend. Standing beside Dorothea was a dark, handsome man with a Byronic look. She had an idea this could only be Dr. Terence Ward.

And so it was. Dorothea introduced them and then left them to enjoy the next waltz together. Not until the dance ended did they have any great opportunity to talk.

The British doctor gazed around him unhappily and said, "Isn't there some smaller room where it would be quieter?"

She smiled at him. "Don't you want to dance?"

"Not right now," he said. "I'd like to get to know you better."

"Very well, then," she told him. "We can try the study."

She led the way from the ballroom and took the shadowed corridor to the study. As she'd hoped, there was a fine log fire blazing in the fireplace and a lighted lamp on one of its tables with the room otherwise in darkness.

The handsome Dr. Terence Ward waited for her to sit in a chair by the fireplace. He stood by the chair, smiling down at her.

"Are you annoyed at my taking you from the dancing?"

"Not at all," she said. "We can still hear the music in the background and this will give us a most important rest for the balance of the night ahead."

He nodded, a handsome figure in his white tie and tails. "When we shall see the New Year in."

"Yes," she said. "Do you mind being in a foreign country at such an important moment?"

"I'm sure I shall enjoy it," the British doctor said. "More especially now, since I have you to keep me company."

He went on to ask her about herself and her life in Philadelphia. She, in turn, questioned him about his home in London and his practice there.

She said, "Will you soon be returning to the old country?"

"Within a few months," Dr. Ward said. "I have my work in a London hospital and then there is my family."

"You have children?"

"No," he said. "But I do have a quantity of family around me. My ailing father is with me. He was once a leading surgeon but he has failed greatly since my mother's death. He was many years older then she. And my brother and his wife also share my home with me, along with my sister, who is the oldest of the family. Since the death of my wife she has taken care of the running of my home for me."

"You surely are not alone," she said. "In Philadelphia there are only my uncle and I. And the servants, of course!"

Dr. Ward showed amused interest. "You must live a rather lonely life."

This was true but she had no wish to admit it. She said, "It is quiet but the house is not all that large."

"Then that is the difference," he said. "My London house is a vast white elephant of a place. It is called Willowgate because of the many weeping willows around it. Though it is actually close by the heart of London the estate has a goodly sum of trees and lawns."

"It sounds interesting," she said.

"It is not an elaborate home," the Britisher said modestly, "but it has been in our family for a long time and, as I've said, it is large. In addition to the family and servants I usually have a medical student living with us. Always some young man working under me at the hospital."

"But you have no children of your own to fill the big house," she said. "No wonder you have come to gather a surrogate family around you."

His handsome face shadowed as he stood there in the glow from the burning logs in the fireplace. "I gather that Dorothea told you I am a widower."

"Yes."

"Unhappily my wife died before we had any children. It was a very tragic business and I have made it a point to avoid any discussion of it."

"Of course," she agreed. "There is nothing to be gained by your dwelling on such a tragedy however much you may have loved her."

"Exactly," he said, his brow furrowed. "To put all that behind me was one of my main reasons for taking leave of England for a while."

"What is your particular interest in surgery?" she asked.

"I'm doing research on operating on the brain," Dr. Terence Ward had told her. "Trepanning or drilling holes in the skull has been practiced since the days of prehistoric man. The cave men used it when there was bone pressure on the skull. In the Middle Ages trepanning was performed to let the devil out in cases of epilepsy. It was also a treatment for headaches. And the mortality rate was always high. It is only lately that we have gone beyond that primal stage in brain surgery."

"Please tell me more," she begged him.

The Byronic-looking surgeon warmed to her interest. He said, "Until a while ago we knew nothing of the inner workings of the brain. In 1861, Paul Broca demonstrated that there was a link between specific areas of the brain and specific movements of the body. Sir William Macewen, under whom I studied surgery in Glasgow, did some pioneer work in brain surgery. He successfully removed the dura mater which covers the brain and did some clever operations to remove blood clots pressing on the brain."

"And now?"

"We are really moving ahead fast," the handsome doctor told her. "Two years ago Victor Horsely, a countryman of mine, began a study of brain anatomy. After animal experimentation he performed ten operations for tumors and epilepsy; one patient died of post operative shock but the others recovered."

Susan suddenly remembered a familiar name from her own background and asked him, "Do you know Dr. William Williams Keen of Philadelphia?"

He reacted with pleased surprise, "Of course I know Dr. Keen!"

"He is a friend of my uncle Charles," she said.

"What a small world it is!" the young doctor exclaimed. "Last year he accomplished one of the most celebrated brain operations to date. He found the site of a tumor by making a hole one and a half inches in diameter in the skull, but this proved to be too small to remove the tumor. With bone clippers Keen managed to widen the aperture until it measured three inches by two and a half. Then he cut through the dura mater and exposed the brain itself. The tumor lay on the surface of the brain and Keen slipped his little finger under it and lifted it out as one scoops an egg from a shell. The patient is alive and a few months ago I saw the tumor preserved in alcohol in the Jefferson Medical College in Philadelphia."

"So you have been in Philadelphia as well!"

"Yes."

"You must come again before you go back home to England," she insisted. "My uncle Charles would enjoy meeting you and entertaining you and Dr. Keen."

Dr. Ward smiled, "Thank you for the invitation. I shall surely try to find time for the visit."

"And I shall call upon Dr. Keen and tell of our meeting at the first opportunity after I return home," she said.

"How long do you plan to remain in Boston?" he asked.

"Another week perhaps," she said. "I do not want to impose on Dorothea too long."

"I'm sure she's delighted to have you here," he said. "And I think we've had enough talk about surgery. Let us return to the ball!"

The party was at its height when they entered the brightly lighted and decorated room again. The wide, swirling skirts of the ladies and the flying black tails of the men's dress coats made patterns in the air as the orchestra played on gaily. She and the handsome doctor were caught up in the joyous mood and soon were dancing as energetically as all the others.

Dorothea's father was a tall, stern-looking man. He was standing near the orchestra with his ancient mother seated in a chair by him, a matriarch in black, to watch the party from this vantage point. Suddenly in the midst of a waltz he raised a white-gloved hand and the violinist signaled the orchestra to stop.

Then Dorothea's father mounted the platform with a glass of champagne in his hand and announced, "Be pleased to find yourselves champagne to toast the New Year of 1889. You have but three minutes to prepare for the event!"

There was laughter and excitement among the guests as the ladies gathered in groups with their fans in hand and the men marched to the long, white-clothed table, where glasses of champagne were set out and waiting. Dr. Terence Ward went to fetch glasses for himself and Susan while she remained at the other side of the ballroom with Dorothea.

Behind her fan, Dorothea whispered, "How do you like him?"

"I think he's very nice. And so brilliant!"

"They say he will become one of the famous surgeons of our day," her friend told her.

By this time their escorts had returned with the champagne and all the company stood facing the orchestra stand as Dorothea's father raised his glass and cried, "My friends, I give you 1889!"

Everyone raised his glass to toast the New Year. She smiled at the handsome doctor over her glass and he smiled back. The orchestra began to play "Auld Lang Syne" and all the voices of the assembly joined in the singing of it. At the end there was a happy confusion of embracing and kissing. Susan found herself in the handsome doctor's arms, receiving an ardent kiss from him.

Even though they were surrounded by noisy, frolicking people she felt it a very private moment. While she was in his arms the rest of the room seemed to melt away. Only when he released her did she return to the frenzied excitement of the New Year celebrants.

When the guests moved on to the dining room she took his arm. They sat together for the after-midnight supper and it was there that they made their first appointment to meet again. He invited her to join him at the Parker House, the famous Boston hostelry, for New Year's night dinner and she accepted. It was arranged that they would meet at six. He told her he would call for her with a sleigh.

He said a special good-night to her before he thanked his hosts at the door and left. She stood watching his caped figure as he vanished down the steps into the winter night and thought that it had been probably the most thrilling evening of all her young life!

The next morning before she was out of bed Dorothea came to her room wrapped in her dressing gown. Her friend sat at the foot of her bed and with twinkling eyes asked, "Are you going to see him again?"

Sitting up in bed, Susan laughed. "How did you guess?"

"I was watching you," her friend said. "It is not hard to tell when two people are falling in love."

Susan blushed prettily. "I don't think it's all that serious."

"But you do like him?"

"I do."

Dorothea said, "Mark my words, you'll end up marrying him! I can feel it in my bones."

"Never!" she protested. "I couldn't think of leaving Uncle Charles and going to England."

Dr. Terence Ward arrived for her promptly at six that night. She was all dressed and ready. He helped her down the icy front steps of the fine Beacon Street mansion and into the sleigh. It was already dark and the windows of the Beacon Street houses with their lights showing behind the tiny, snow-mantled panes of glass had a charming look of Christmas.

As he pulled the buffalo robe over them he said, "I've been waiting all day just to have a glimpse of your lovely face once again."

She smiled at his compliment. "I've looked forward to tonight as well."

The driver of the sleigh lost no time in getting them to the Parker House. Here was light and warmth once again. They stepped from the wintry night into the warmth of the red-carpeted and mahogany paneled lobby of the fine hotel. After they had checked their outer clothing a distinguished-looking head waiter ushered them into the chandeliered splendor of the high-ceilinged dining room. Fine paintings looked down on them from the wood paneled walls and the many round, white-clothed tables were almost completely filled with patrons in formal dress.

The head waiter treated the handsome doctor with some deference and seated them at a table not far from the stage at one end where a string quartet was playing soft dinner music.

As they made their selection of food and wine from the menu, he said, "I have grown to like this hotel. It was a favorite of Charles Dickens, you know. He came here on his American tours, right up until the time of his death."

"What a loss that was!" she sighed. "How I love Pickwick!"

The doctor nodded. "One of the greatest of his creations."

Their dinner proceeded. The service was excellent and the pheasant they had chosen went very well with the fine Burgundy. When the dessert course was over they lingered over coffee and brandy.

Dr. Terence Ward offered her a thin smile. "I have no desire to go out into the cold blast of winter again."

"Nor I," she said, dreamily.

"We must meet soon again. I want to know you better before you leave," he said earnestly.

She didn't want to compromise herself or him so she said, "But you must be very busy at the hospital. Can you spare the time?"

"In a case like this. I will spare it," he said.

"I'm very selfish," she told him, "but I would like to see you some more."

"Then it is settled," he said. "I need some rest in any case. Before I left England, after my wife's tragic death, I had a period of illness. I was in private hospital for a time."

"Oh?" She had not heard anything about this before.

He frowned slightly. "It was mostly nerves, of course. But I lost considerable weight and was not able to work for a while."

"But you have fully recovered?"

"Oh, yes," he said quickly. "I'm myself once again. But I thought that coming to America would be a good change for me. It also fitted in with my plans for research over here."

"I'm so glad you did decide to come here," she said. "I know you dislike discussing your wife's death but I find myself wondering what she died of. Believe me it is more than idle curiosity on my part, call it an interest in you and yours."

The handsome doctor looked ill at ease. Then in a taut voice, he said, "Her death came by accident. And it was sudden. She had been in perfect health up to the time it happened."

"How awful!" she sympathized.

"It did not happen in our home," he went on. "She had gone a few blocks away to be with an aunt who was very ill. The accident occurred outside the aunt's house. I wasn't there but they summoned me in due course. She was dead by then!"

"What a tragedy!" she said, picturing a street accident in which some heavy vehicle had knocked down the unfortunate woman and ran over her. Such dreadful accidents were happening every day in the great cities.

"I had been visiting a postoperative patient who'd had a relapse and bad bleeding. I was busy most of the night with him. The hospital finally located me at his house and then I went to my wife. I still feel pain when I recall the dreadful moment of finding her dead."

"I'm sorry," she said. "You mustn't talk about it any more. I was only curious as to what her illness had been. Now you have explained we must never discuss it again."

His look of gratitude was touching. "Thank you, Susan," he said. "I do want to call you Susan."

"I am your friend," she said gently.

"You must call me Terry," he said. "That is how I'm known to all my friends."

She smiled. "Terry! I like that! So much less formal than Terence!"

"You must take my good wishes to Dr. Keen when you return to Philadelphia," he said.

"And you must keep to your word and come and visit us," she reminded him.

As it happened he did keep his word. He'd all but proposed to her before she took the train back to Philadelphia. And in the letters which they wrote each other almost daily they came to the point of discussing marriage. Susan made a bargain that if her uncle Charles approved of him she would marry him. And so it stood when the handsome and energetic Dr. Terence Ward arrived in February for the promised visit with her.

Her uncle Charles at once took to the young man. His friend Dr. Keen also met and approved of him. Susan's young doctor became a favorite guest of the most socially elect Philadelphians. It was not hard to guess that her uncle would encourage her to marry the young British surgeon.

"You're not likely to find a more handsome fellow or a more brilliant one, if Dr. Keen is right," her uncle told her. "I'd like to see you settled with a good husband. I'm an old man, I can't tell how long I may have."

"Nonsense, Uncle Charles," she'd protested. "You'll live for years yet."

"We both know that's not true," Uncle Charles said. "And if this young man asks me for your hand I'll surely give him my blessing."

And he did! Terry proposed to Susan and it was arranged to have the wedding in Philadelphia in late March.

Following the wedding she and Terry would return to England. She quickly wrote to Dorothea inviting her to come to Philadelphia and be her maid of honor. She felt her solicitous Boston friend deserved it for working so hard to keep her from becoming a spinster.

Terry returned to Boston to complete his research work at the hospital there. In the meanwhile she'd found herself caught up in a whirl of wedding preparations. It was a time of frantic preparation. They would be sailing for England shortly after the marriage and she would have no time to gather together a wardrobe then. So it all had to be done before the wedding.

In the mornings she saw the seamstress and in the afternoons she looked after the thousand and one other details, including seeing the clergyman who was to perform the ceremony. The Rev. Isaac Mullen had not met Terry during his visit to Philadelphia but he took an active interest in him and his background.

When Susan met with him in the vestry to discuss the wedding the old clergyman said, "As I understand it Dr. Ward is a widower."

"Yes. That is true."

The old man's sharp eyes studied her from beneath shaggy white brows. "What caused her death?"

"An accident, I believe."

"Very sad," the old man said. "What sort of accident?"

She hesitated, uneasily. "I'm not altogether sure. He doesn't like to discuss it."

"Oh?" the old clergyman showed mild surprise.

Susan felt her cheeks burn. It was hard to explain how sensitive Terry was on the subject. She said, "I believe it was a street accident."

"Ah, a street accident!" the old clergyman echoed her.

"Yes. She'd been in good health up to then so it was a great shock to the doctor."

"Naturally. She was killed at once?"

"Yes. I gather that. She was dead when he reached her side. We have made a mutual agreement not to discuss it. So I would appreciate your not mentioning it."

"Indeed?" the old clergyman looked hesitant. Then he said, "Well if that is your wish. I felt I should know the details of his first wife's death."

"And now you do," she said.

"Yes, I do, at least in a general sense," he agreed.

The wedding was a brilliant success and the reception which followed had Philadelphia talking for weeks. Dr. Keen proposed the toast to the bride and her uncle gave them a handsome cash gift. It seemed that before she knew it Terry had whisked her off to New York to spend a little time until their sailing for London.

It was in New York that she first worried about him.

Though they thoroughly enjoyed their honeymoon in the city there were several times when he'd left her and been absent for hours. When he returned he was usually in an elated mood and full of apologies. Invariably he'd encountered some medical colleague on the street or in a restaurant and gone off to visit a hospital with him. It was difficult for her to reprimand him for these long absences with his offering so reasonable an explanation.

But now as she lay in bed in this London hotel room, staring up into the darkness, she began to wonder if these absences had been but preludes leading up to his disappearance from their room in the middle of the night. Was there a side to her husband's nature which he was hiding from her? Was she unaware of some defect in his character which made him absent himself from her in this manner? Was he really in as good health as he'd insisted? All these questions plagued her as she lay awake waiting for his return. At last sheer exhaustion made her close her eyes and she slept.

Chapter Two

When Susan opened her eyes the first thing she saw was her husband standing by one of the windows with the drapes held slightly back as he gazed down into the street. He was fully dressed and his back was to her as he gave his attention to the window.

"Terry!" she exclaimed, sitting up in bed.

He turned to her at once allowing the drape to fall closed and placing the room in faint shadow again although it was obviously morning. The next thing she noticed about him was that he was unusually pale and seemed rather nervous.

Coming over to her bedside he bent and kissed her tenderly on the lips. "Good morning, Susan," he said.

She gazed up at him worriedly. "I woke in the night and found you gone. I was half out of my mind with worry about you! Where have you been?"

Her handsome husband stood by her bed looking uncomfortable. "I'm sorry. I didn't want to wake you."

"But where were you?"

"A colleague of mine, Dr. Donald Farrow, came here in the middle of the night. A patient of his was dying from post-operative complications. Dr. Farrow learned that I was in London and came here to get my help. You didn't waken when he knocked on our door or when I talked with him. So I was able to dress and leave quietly without disturbing you. My hope was to get back before you woke up. I'm sorry that I didn't."

She listened with a feeling of relief. "Why didn't you

waken me?" she said. "I would have preferred that to waking alone and finding you'd vanished!"

"I made a mistake," he said. "I'm sorry."

"Were you able to help the patient?" she asked.

"I made certain suggestions and he is still alive."

She gave him an admiring smile. "Then I cannot quarrel with you for what you did. What is more noble than saving lives?"

"I won't guarantee this life has been saved," he told her. "But I have done my best."

"Is it still foggy?" she asked.

"I regret that it is," her handsome husband said. "You will have to adapt yourself to our London fogs. When the weather is good, it is ideal and somehow makes up for spells such as this."

"I wish it were a sunny day," she sighed. "It is the day when I shall first enter my new home."

Terence said, "You mustn't worry about it. I'll go order breakfast while you are dressing. And we shall have a cozy meal up here before we leave."

She told him what she'd like and he went down to place the order. In the meanwhile she hurried and washed and dressed. His explanation of his absence had completely satisfied her and she reproached herself for having been suspicious about his vanishing. She'd only felt that way because of the several times he'd left her without explanation while they were in New York. Now it was all settled in her mind.

She opened the drapes and let the gray, fog-ridden daylight into the room a few minutes before a waiter arrived with a breakfast tray. While the elderly waiter was setting the breakfast out her husband returned with a paper under his arm.

She said, "I see you have the morning paper. What is the news?"

His handsome face showed a wan smile. "Really nothing you'd be interested in. The Queen has returned from Scotland to Windsor Castle. That is news over here."

"It would seem I shall have to cultivate an interest in royalty," she said good-humoredly.

He carefully folded the paper and placed it by one of their unopened suitcases. The waiter had finished setting out breakfast and they sat down at the table. Susan was becoming familiar with the hearty English breakfasts. Spread before her were dishes of potted beef, roast fowl, ham, tongue, and anchovies, along with milk, cream, eggs, muffins, and tea.

Her husband helped himself to the potted beef and roast fowl while she settled for the more familiar bacon and eggs. All the food was warm and delicious. She was taking a sip of her tea when she first noticed the stain on the inner side of the arm of her husband's jacket. He was wearing a smartly cut jacket of gray tweed and at the cuff there was this dark stain about the size of a half-dollar.

She put down her cup and said, "You've a stain on your right sleeve!"

He showed surprise. "On my sleeve?"

"Yes. Your right sleeve on the inside."

He touched a napkin to his lips with his left hand and glanced at the stain. It was dark and unpleasant looking. He frowned and said, "I was in the hotel bar briefly last night. Someone stupidly upset a drink and I accidentally let my sleeve get in the mess. I remember the chap next to me spilled a liqueur and ordered another. That had to be when it happened."

"What a shame!" she said. "I like that jacket. I'll try and clean the spot after breakfast."

"No," her husband said hurriedly. "Let me attend to it while you pack. I don't want to lose any time and I have some experience with stains."

"Just as you like," she said. "You're very edgy this morning."

"Am I?" he looked upset.

"Yes," she said. "It is not good for you to get up in the middle of the night and struggle to save patients' lives. You should be firm about such things. Remember you are recovering from an illness and you should be more careful of yourself."

He offered her a shade of a smile. "I'll try and remember that."

"As my husband, you may depend on me to take a hand in this," she said firmly. "I will not let you wreck your health."

Her doctor husband reached across the table and gave her hand a warm squeeze. "What a beautiful little protector I have found for myself. I had no idea you'd be so concerned."

"It is my duty to protect the one I love," she said. "You will find that we American girls have minds of our own."

"So it would seem," he said, letting her hand go. "But as a medical man there are certain calls which I cannot ignore."

They finished breakfast and she busied herself with packing her bags. Their trunks had already been sent ahead to Willowgate so the luggage they had with them was only for day-to-day use and for the purchases they'd made in London. While she did this her husband briefly vanished and returned with another jacket on.

He said, "I had very poor luck with the stain so I have packed the jacket away and put on this one. Some time later we can try to do something about cleaning it."

"I hope it can be cleaned," she said. "That was one of my favorite jackets. You looked so handsome in it."

Terence smiled and asked, "Do I look so ugly in this?"

"Not at all," she said. "In fact you are handsome in my eyes regardless of what you wear."

He laughed and embraced her. Then he said, "Now I shall call the porters to take our things down. I ordered the carriage for this hour."

There was the usual bustle and confusion in the next few minutes. But at last they arrived at the door of the pleasant hotel where the coachman began loading their bags into the closed carriage which he'd brought for them. As they stood in the doorway of the hotel she shivered at the cold dampness of the foggy day and was thankful that the ride to her new home would be made in a closed vehicle.

The sidewalk was teeming with a passing parade of people. Men in black top hats on their way to business predominated in the group. In the street there was a continuous tangle of carriages, wagons, and drays. A noisy hubbub of loud voices and creaking wheels filled the air.

Standing just outside the entrance of the hotel was a news vendor with his stock of papers under his arm. "Morning paper," he shouted stridently. "Another horrible murder! Murder! Mutilation! Murder!"

A stout man came and bought a paper. He opened it and in an aside to his companion said loudly enough for her to overhear, "It's Jack the Ripper again! Claims his third victim!" The two moved on.

Her husband had also overheard and when she turned to glance at him she saw a strangely tense expression on his handsome face and he'd suddenly gone very white.

Taking her almost roughly by the arm, he said, "Come, it is time to get in the coach!"

She allowed him to propel her across the sidewalk to the vehicle. She settled. back on the horsehair seat and noted the odor of the stables which filled the shadowed interior of the carriage. Her husband gave some instructions to the driver and then got in beside her and closed the door.

As the vehicle started on its way she turned to him and said, "I thought you told me there was nothing much in the morning paper." He frowned slightly. "In my opinion it was sadly lacking in news."

She said, "What about the murder? The one the news vendor was shouting about just now. Who is Jack the Ripper?"

Dr. Ward looked grim. "I'm sorry you heard all that."

"Why?"

"I hoped to spare you from learning anything about it."

"But I want to hear about it," she insisted. "I think I should know what is happening in London since it is where I'm going to live."

"This has to do with a dark side of the city with which I trust you will never come in contact," he said.

"Who is Jack the Ripper? You haven't told me."

"No one knows," he said.

"What is known about him?"

Her husband shrugged. "He murders women in the streets at night. The killings began with the murder of Mary Ann Nicholas on the night of August 31 in 1888. They have been going on ever since. The murder last night makes at least the third or fourth victim. No one quite sure of the number."

"But how do the authorities know the killings are the work of one individual?"

Her husband gave her a weary glance. "Must you have all the details?"

"Yes. You should have let me read the paper."

He scowled and in a rather toneless voice recited, "The victims have been chiefly streetwalkers of the most degraded type. The murders have usually taken place outdoors. The women are lured or dragged into a dark alley. There in the shadows he cuts their throats with a knife and indulges his mania for other mutilations of the body."

"Other mutilations!" she gasped.

"Yes. Apparently this Jack the Ripper uses a long-handled knife and has a degree of anatomical knowledge. All his victims thus far have been killed in the same fashion."

"And he is still at large?"

"It would seem so, judging by last night's murder."

"Where did it take place?"

"In a squalid place called Miller's Court," her husband said. "I really don't want to talk about it any more!"

"Just one more question; haven't the police been able to find any suspects?"

"A number of persons have been detained and questioned," he said. "A Polish immigrant, an American sailor, and even a Russian doctor. They believe it has to be someone with a knowledge of surgery or someone with a butcher's background."

"I see," she said.

"Now let us forget this dark subject and talk about your arrival at our home," her husband said. "I wish to prepare you for the various people you will meet there."

"Very well," she said as the carriage moved on through the foggy streets.

"The house is in Elgin Street," he said. "And one of our neighbors is my colleague, Dr. Donald Farrow. He is older than I am and a bachelor who lives with his sister. You will often see him as he visits with us regularly."

She said, "He is the one who called you out last night."

Her husband hesitated slightly as if he'd forgotten. He said, "Ah, yes. But that is not important for the moment. Our bedroom and adjoining parlor are on the second floor of the house and at the rear overlooking the garden with its central fountain. The fountain is iron and impressive. The figures of nymphs which support it were molded in iron and brought here from Italy."

"It sounds very nice," she said.

"Now about the people in the house," he went on. "First, there is my father, Dr. Simon Ward. He was once recognized as the finest surgeon in London but he is a very old man now and suffering from senility—so much so that he is largely confined to an attic apartment with Baker, one of the oldest of our male servants, as his keeper."

"How tragic!" she said.

"It is," Terence Ward agreed. "He does have days when he is fairly lucid and then Baker brings him down to join the rest of us. But there are other times when his memory and mind are blank. Then there is my brother, Phillip, and his wife Angelica. Phillip started out to be a surgeon but failed. He has gone into the business of supplying surgical supplies to the many hospitals in England and has built a prosperous firm. His wife is an attractive woman, younger than Phillip, and very ambitious."

"Phillip is younger than you?" she asked.

"No. Older by six years," he said. "He proposed to and married Angelica after I married Ruth."

It was one of the few times she'd heard him mention his late first wife. She said, "And what about your sister?"

"Samantha is the oldest of us three," Terence Ward said. "She is beyond the age when she is likely to marry now. She kept house for my father after my mother's death, and because she was older than Phillip and I she became something of a mother to us. Now she runs the affairs of our household, but you shall help her of course."

"What about your brother's wife?" she asked. "Mustn't she feel frustrated, taking second place to two other women in the house?"

"No," he said. "She has a great many outside interests. She has bowed to Phillip's wish to share my father's household as long as he is alive. Phillip feels the family should all be together."

Her eyes widened. "Then Willowgate is really your father's house?"

"I prefer to regard it as the family's house," he corrected her.

She shrugged, "Well, in either case it is about the same thing."

"Aside from the servants those are the people you'll be meeting when we arrive at the house," he said.

"There are no children?"

"Phillip and Angelica had a son and lost it," he said. "And I do not believe Angelica wants another child. She has many social activities and she is an excellent archer and bicyclist, a true sportswoman."

"I see," she said.

"There is one person I've forgotten," he said. "And a young man too important to be overlooked. His name is Oliver Rush and he is an intern under me at the hospital."

"You mentioned that you almost always had a student doctor living with you in the house."

"It works out very well," he said. "There are occasions when someone like Oliver Rush can answer an emergency in my place. Also it places him in almost constant contact with me and he is able to adopt a professional viewpoint more quickly."

"I can see that," she agreed. In hearing the brief histories of the people she was soon to meet she'd temporarily forgotten the dark news of Jack the Ripper and his latest victim of the night before.

They reached a house set in from the street with an iron railing having spiked points guarding its grounds. The carriage turned in on a gravel driveway and passed by rows of huge light green weeping willows to come upon a giant, square, red-brick house with vine-covered walls and its windows and entrance door trimmed in white. She recognized it as Willowgate from the many descriptions her husband had given her of it.

It was surely not an attractive house and yet it was an impressive one. The word brooding had almost come into her mind as she tried to find the proper adjective for it. No sign of life showed as they came to a halt before its door.

Terry turned to her with a relieved look. "Well, here we are! At last the family will see my lovely bride!"

She blushed and felt distinctly nervous. The moment of meeting her new family had come upon her more swiftly than she'd expected. She said, "I hope I measure up to your descriptions of me."

"You'll do even better than that," he assured her as he got out of the coach and helped her down.

As she advanced to the door of Willowgate with her husband she experienced a feeling of fear. At the moment she blamed it on her uneasiness about the reception she might get from his relatives, but later she was to acknowledge that it was due more to the grim old mansion itself. Willowgate exerted this dark influence over her right from the beginning.

The door opened and an elderly manservant came out. He bowed to them and smiled. "Welcome home, Mr. Terence!"

"Good to see you, Baker," her husband said heartily. "This is my wife." And to her he added, "This is Baker, of whom I spoke earlier."

She smiled at the old servant. "Of course. How do you do, Baker."

"Very well, Mrs. Ward," he said with a bow. "Welcome to Willowgate." And he then went to fetch their bags as they entered the reception hall of the red-brick house.

A tall, spare woman in a black dress emerged from the shadows of the reception hall to greet them. Her thin face bore a slight resemblance to Terence and Susan instantly guessed this had to be his sister, Samantha.

Samantha opened her arms to her and said, "I hope you will be very happy here, Susan!"

Terence stood by and asked, "Where are the others?"

"Phillip had to go to the city on business and Oliver Rush is at the hospital," she said. "But Angelica and Father are waiting in the drawing room to meet your new bride."

Terence frowned slightly. "I saw that Baker was downstairs. Is father all right today?"

Samantha's pinched face showed pain. "He is not as well as we might wish but he is fairly rational. And he did so want to meet Susan."

Terence turned to Susan with a sigh. "I suppose we must go through with it. I hope it's not too much of an ordeal for you, my dear."

"It will be all right," she said. "I understand your father is not well."

"You'll see our things are put in our apartment," Terence said to his sister.

"Yes. I'm waiting to tell Baker what to do with them," Samantha said.

"Very well," Terence said grimly. "We'll go in and face the music. Come along, Susan."

They crossed the hall and went into the huge, high-ceilinged drawing room. Its wood-paneled walls were dark and maintained the impression of gloom, which seemed to be the predominant note about the old house. The ceiling was beamed in dark wood and there were prints and paintings on the walls. It was well filled with heavy antique furniture and at one end there was a fireplace in which logs were blazing. Over the fireplace hung a full-length portrait of a lovely young, dark-haired woman in a flowing white gown. The glow from the fireplace provided a kind of lighting for the painting.

Standing by the fireplace was a blond young woman whom Susan judged not to be much older than herself. She knew this had to be Angelica and she was startled that she should be so near her own age since she was married to Terence's older brother. The girl had a cold, chiseled sort of beauty—the only marring touch a rather long nose. Her eyes were blue and shrewd and she seemed to Susan to be carefully appraising her as she approached.

In a chair before the blazing logs of the fireplace sat hunched a very old-looking man with a short white beard and white hair with a bald spot on top. He turned as she drew near and she was startled to see in the emaciated, bearded face a direct resemblance to her husband. It was a bizarre experience to see this wasted, sallow face which must have once been as handsome as Terence's.

Terence went directly to his father and touched a hand to his shoulder. "Father!" he said warmly. And then he crossed to the blond Angelica and kissed her on the cheek gently. "It is good to see you again, my dear," he said.

Angelica smiled and was obviously pleased with his greeting. "And to see you, dear Terence. I'm sorry Phillip had to be in the city, but he promised to return early."

"Good," Terence said. He turned to his wife. "This is Susan!"

"How do you do," she said shyly to them both.

Angelica came forward to her at once and took her in her arms for a kiss of greeting. Susan noted how cool her flesh was and that she smelled of a delicate lavender.

"Welcome to Willowgate," the blond young woman said.

"Thank you," she said.

Old Dr. Simon Ward had struggled to his feet and was standing there rather shakily, his somewhat bulging eyes a shade too bright as he smiled and revealed yellow fangs of teeth.

"So you are the bride," he said in a quavering voice.

"Yes," she said. "I hope you will look on me as a daughter."

The old man chuckled and with a trembling yet surprisingly strong hand drew her close and then kissed her. He said, "I'm a doctor, too, you know."

"Yes, Terry told me," she said, somewhat repulsed by the not entirely clean old man and taking a step away from him and closer to her husband.

Terence looked slightly annoyed. He said, "You can rest easy, Father. I have told her you are the most gifted surgeon in the house. I can never match you!"

The bearded wreckage of a man continued to stand there weaving slightly. "I was in the Crimea, you know! Served in the Crimea for the Queen! It takes a war to make a surgeon! I learned a lot over there!"

"I'm sure you did," she said.

"Operating in the field!" the old man ranted. "That's where you learned to wield a knife! Amputations by the dozens! Bleeding to death! Cauterize! None of your namby-pamby of your London Hospital operating rooms! That was surgery!"

A frown crossed her husband's face and he moved quickly

to his father. "You're upsetting yourself needlessly, Father," he said. "There is plenty of time to tell Susan about your experiences later."

The old man gave him a hostile look and slumped down into his chair. "You want to deny me!" he accused Terence.

"I want to do nothing of the sort!" her husband said.

"You'll never handle a knife like me," the old man told him. "The Queen decorated me for bravery in the field. You hear that, new bride?"

"Yes. I'm sure everyone is very proud of you," she said.

The sallow, bearded face registered disgust at this. "Proud of me? Proud of the old madman they lock in the attic! There's none of them appreciate me and they'll turn you against me!"

"Now you're talking nonsense, Father Ward," Angelica said, joining in the conversation again.

The old man in the chair glared at her. "I know you and I know my precious sons! If it weren't for Samantha you'd have me locked in an asylum somewhere. As it is I've only been shut in the attic!"

"This is no way for you to talk during Susan's first meeting with you," Terry protested. "What sort of person is she going to think you?"

The old man stared at him blankly. "Susan?"

"Yes, my wife," Terence said. "You shouldn't say such things before her."

"Your wife is Ruth," the old man said. "Don't lie to me! I know her name!"

Susan saw the distressed look on her husband's face and at once felt sorry for him. It was clear that the old man's mind was clouding as it apparently often did. He'd already forgotten his introduction to her when he'd seemed quite familiar with her name.

"Susan!" Terence corrected his father almost angrily.

She touched her husband's arm. "Don't let it bother you! I understand!"

The old man in the chair was staring at her in an odd way. "Ruth!" he said in his harsh voice. "Ruth, come back from the dead! We don't often see you in the daylight!"

"Father!" her husband said reproachfully. And he went to the old man and helped him out of the chair. "It is time to go to your room now."

The bearded Simon Ward nodded grimly. "Lock me up! Old madman! Talk too much!"

Terence made no reply to this. He took the old man by the arm and led him past Susan on the way out of the room. The expression on her husband's face was tormented as he went by. She felt a wave of compassion for him as she did for the old man who stumbled along at his side mumbling incoherently.

She called after them, "Good-bye, Father Ward."

There was no answer from either of the men as Terence had difficulty getting his protesting father out of the drawing room. Susan turned to Angelica and saw that the blond young woman was giving her a cool, amused look.

Angelica asked, "Does he frighten you?"

"Not really," she said.

"He should," her sister-in-law warned. "I think he might be violent on occasion. And he doesn't seem to have gotten you properly placed."

"It's sad to see so clever a man reduced to that state," she said.

The cool blonde said, "Age does that to most people. I let Samantha croon over him. She enjoys being a martyr to her father and see what it has gotten her. Nothing! When he dies she'll be an unwanted old maid."

Susan said, "I'm glad to meet you, Angelica. I had no idea you'd be as young and attractive as you are."

The other girl showed ironical amusement. "Because I happen to be married to Terry's older brother?"

"Yes. I suppose so."

"As a matter of fact," Angelica said, "Terry courted me before Phillip did. It seemed that we were going to be married and then he met Ruth."

This was surprising news. She said, "Oh?"

Angelica sat in one of the easy chairs and draped her fancy rose gown with its white lace trim so that it wouldn't wrinkle. It was clear that she took pride in her clothes.

The blond girl said, "After that I saw very little of Terry until one day he came to me and told me he was in love with Ruth and intended to marry her."

"I see," she said quietly, still standing before the fireplace.

"I wasn't exactly happy," Angelica said. "I didn't think Ruth would make him a good wife. I was sure they'd continually be at odds. But there is no reasoning with a man in love." Her smile was mocking. "I'm sure you understand that."

"I'm sure there's a great deal of truth in the saying."

"I promise you there is," the girl in the chair said. "So he married her and they were never all that happy. Then Phillip came to me and asked me if I'd accept him as second choice. That's the funny thing about Phillip. He can never see himself as an important member of the family, and he is. He has this nervous attitude where the family is concerned and he's not at all like that in business."

"Why is that?"

Angelica shrugged. "I'd guess it is because he failed as a surgeon. He had no stomach for it and didn't complete his

studies. His father berated him for disgracing the family repu-
tation and then Terry came along and showed a great apti-
tude as a surgeon and became the golden lad of the family.
Phillip has never recovered from that."

"But you say he has been a success in business?"

"He's made a great deal more money than Terry,"
Angelica said. "He is the largest supplier of surgical needs in
the city."

"Then he should feel satisfied," she said.

"He doesn't," Angelica told her. "He has kept all his textbooks and even his case of instruments. Sometimes at night
he sits studying those textbooks and taking out the instruments and polishing them. It's so silly and pointless. Why
does he care now that his father is no longer able to condemn
him?"

"Have you tried to talk to him about it?"

"There's no reasoning with him," Angelica declared.
"I've looked at the textbooks many a time and they repulse
me!" She shuddered. "Those gory illustrations!"

"But you and Phillip are happy?"

"As happy as we expected to be," she said in her cool way.
"He knows I wouldn't have chosen him before Terry and
that's that. But we manage."

Susan was finding it hard to understand the cold blonde.

It seemed to her that Angelica would be bound to resent
her since she still must be more than half in love with Terry.

She said, "I always felt that Terry and his first wife were
ideally happy."

"Not all the time."

"Was she very lovely?"

Angelica gave her another of those mocking glances.
"Why don't you decide for yourself? That's her portrait just
in front of you."

Susan hadn't been prepared for this. She stared up at the life-size portrait of the beautiful dark-haired girl. "So that's Ruth," she said.

"Yes. Terry had it painted just before her death."

"I'd say she was truly beautiful," Susan said still studying the portrait above the fireplace.

"Most people thought so."

"Her face shows a sadness," Susan said. "Almost as if she knew she must soon die."

"She had no knowledge of it at all."

"I understand she met her death through an accident," she said.

"Yes," Angelica said with another of those mocking looks. "That is how it happened."

"Terry hasn't told me much about her or how she met her death," she confessed.

"Really?" the blond girl raised her eyebrows.

"No," she said awkwardly. "It seems to be too painful a matter for him to cope with. So I haven't pressed him."

"I expect he approves of that."

"I guess so," she said. "He did tell me that Ruth had gone to the city to nurse a dying aunt."

"That is correct."

"And the accident happened there."

"Yes."

Susan sighed. "Terry told me that by the time he'd heard about it and reached her she was dead."

"I'm sure she was dead even before that," Angelica, said. "I think she must have been killed instantly."

"I've had so few details," she said.

Angelica was staring at her in an odd way. "I find that strange. That Terry hasn't wanted to tell you about it."

Susan smiled forlornly. "I respected his wishes in the

matter. If it pains him to recall it, better that it isn't discussed."

"I disagree," the blond Angelica said. "I think Terry ought to have been frank with you. He ought to have told you how Ruth met her death. The kind of accident she had!"

There was something in the other girl's tone which bothered her. In a faint voice, she asked, "What sort of accident was it?"

"She was murdered."

"Murdered!"

"Yes," her sister-in-law said coldly. "The general opinion seems to be she was a victim of Jack the Ripper."

Chapter Three

The blond girl's words came as a complete shock to her. She repeated in a taut voice, "Jack the Ripper!"

"Surely you had some inkling of this," Angelica said.

"No!"

"I'm sorry, then," she said. "I had no intention of upsetting you so soon after your arrival here." Yet there was a hint of smugness of tone which suggested this was exactly what might have been the case.

Susan glanced up at the portrait of Terence's first wife and said, "She was so lovely!"

"Murderers seldom show mercy in that regard," Angelica said in her cold fashion. "You know about the Jack the Ripper murders, of course?"

Susan gave the other girl a frightened glance. "I first knew there were a series of such murders this morning. There was another one last night."

"Really?" Angelica showed interest. "I had not heard about it."

"It was in the morning newspapers."

"That must have been very shocking to Terry," Angelica said. "Hardly a nice welcome to London for him."

"He didn't want to talk about it," she admitted. "But I did drag some information from him."

"Of course you had no idea that Ruth was supposed to be one of Jack the Ripper's victims?"

"No. He hadn't told me. He said she'd died of an accident while on a visit to a sick aunt in another part of the city."

"The part about visiting a sick aunt in another part of the city was true enough," Angelica said. "As for the accident part, Ruth was murdered when she set out on an errand to find another nurse for her aunt. Her errand took her into a dark courtyard and it was there that she was attacked and murdered in the fashion peculiar to Jack the Ripper."

Susan was still stunned by these revelations. She asked, "What makes it possible to link all these murders?"

"They appear to be the work of someone with surgical knowledge," Angelica said, repeating in part what she'd already heard from Terry. "In fact, the authorities believe that the killer is either a surgeon or has had some sort of surgical training. He mutilates his victims with a surgeon's precision."

"How dreadful!" she gasped.

"For a while the papers were full of it. It was very hard on Terry. You see some of the murders have taken place not far from here."

"Oh?"

"Yes," Angelica went on. "At least two of them did. And then Ruth lived here in the same area and it was suggested she might have been trailed to her aunt's place by the murderer. Since Terry has been away there has been a lull in the murders. I find it ironic that they should begin again now that he has returned."

"That is very strange," Susan said tensely. She was thinking about her husband's strange reaction to the news of the murder and his absence from their bedroom during the time when the murder must have been committed.

"Even Queen Victoria has written to the papers urging the police to find the monster guilty of these crimes," the blond girl said. "But so far it has done no good. At the time of Ruth's murder we actually had the police here investigating."

"Here?" she gasped.

"Of course! They questioned all of us. I began to wonder if they suspected someone in this house."

Her eyes widened in fear. "Why would you think that?"

Angelica shrugged. "There are so many individuals living here with surgical knowledge. And Jack the Ripper is claimed to have such knowledge. I personally was suspicious of the young medical student living here at that time."

"Indeed?" Susan was at once grateful her sister-in-law had mentioned the medical student rather than Terry or someone else in the house.

"Yes. They questioned him a great deal. He and Terry had a falling-out soon after Ruth's murder and the student left here. Later he hung himself in his new lodgings."

"He killed himself?" she asked in awe.

"It created another sensation!" Angelica said. "And I thought then that perhaps he was Jack the Ripper. I believe the police had the same feeling. Especially as the killings ended after that. But if they began again last night it would seem that theory is wrong."

Susan said, "Why would the student kill himself?"

"I haven't the faintest notion," Angelica said. "But I have heard my husband, Phillip, discuss the case and he says that every year a small percentage of medical students take their own lives. It appears that some of them are unsuited to the profession and the strain of their training is more than they can endure."

"I see," she said quietly.

"In any case the killings have started again," the blond girl said. "You must be very cautious. Don't stray far from the house when you're alone. I have been most vigilant since Ruth's murder."

"I can well understand," she agreed.

"We have another young doctor living here now, Oliver Rush. But he is not the neurotic type. We are all very fond of him."

"Thank you for being so frank with me," she said, still worrying about it all. Though the information about the previous medical student and his suicide had helped ease her mind about whether her own husband might be mixed in the frightful business or not.

"You mustn't be frightened," Angelica said.

"Frightened of what?" It was a somewhat irate Dr. Terence Ward who put this question to his sister-in-law. He had entered the room quietly without their being aware of it to only now make his presence known to them.

Angelica at once rose to her feet with an uneasy look on her attractive face. "I was telling Susan not to be afraid of this brooding old house," she said.

"Really?" There was sarcasm and distrust in her husband's tone.

"Yes," Angelica said. "I was only trying to be helpful."

"I'm sure you were!" Terry's look was grim and his tone held a note of stinging sarcasm. He turned to Susan and said, "I'd like to show you our apartment now."

"Of course," she said.

"You'll excuse us?" he said to Angelica.

She nodded without saying anything and remained standing under the portrait of the murdered first wife of Dr. Terence Ward. It struck Susan that the blond girl seemed extremely forlorn.

Susan accompanied her husband up the stairs considering all that she'd just heard. It gave an entirely new aspect to her marriage and to Terence Ward himself. She determined to attempt to keep these new apprehensions private.

They arrived at the second floor and she was impressed by

the darkness of the corridors; she put this down partly to the drab wallpapers used in the old mansion. Her feet sank in the heavy carpeting on the hardwood floor and all was very silent. They went down a short hallway and her handsome husband stood by an open door.

"This is the entrance to our apartment," he said in his serious fashion.

She rather timidly approached the door and entered an ornate parlor. It was decorated in a dark gray shade with a lot of overstuffed furniture, a handsome Persian rug and a white marble fireplace at one end of the big room. Once again she felt the room to be luxurious yet oppressive.

"It is very elegant," she managed.

"You think so?" Her handsome husband was watching her closely and she thought there was irony in his tone.

"Yes. Did you select the furnishings?"

"No. My sister Samantha did. She is responsible for most of the decorating of the house."

"I see," she said, thinking that she might have guessed this. The rather drab Samantha had truly decorated Willowgate in her own image.

"Now on to the bedroom," Terence said.

She went to the open door at the end of the room and made her way into the bedroom. It was almost as large as the parlor and had a huge double bed with a canopy above it. This room was done in blue and white, and the canopy was of pale blue. Standing by the dresser was a pleasant-looking, thin girl with yellow hair in pigtails, wearing the black dress and white apron of a maid.

"This is Sally," Terence said, introducing her to the girl. "She will be your personal maid." To the girl, he said, "Sally, this is your new mistress."

"Welcome, madam," Sally said, with a tiny curtsy.

"Thank you, Sally," she said with a small smile for the girl.

"I have unpacked some of your things," the girl told her. "Shall I remain and continue or come back later?"

"You may return later," Dr. Terence Ward said, taking the matter into his own hands.

"Very well, sir," the girl said rather nervously and curtsied and hurried out of the room to leave them alone.

He turned to Susan and asked, "Well, are you satisfied with it?"

"It's very nice," she said, glancing around her and seeing a potted palm by the window which she felt too heavy and which also cut off light from the room. "I shall probably make a few changes to suit my own tastes."

"By all means," her husband agreed.

She moved across to the window and gazed out. Terry had properly described the view of the garden with its cast-iron fountain. The undoubtedly attractive garden was also made drab by the gray fog which still mantled the area.

She said, "There is a lovely view."

"I told you that," he said.

She turned to him, "It should be very nice on a fine day."

"Yes," he said, those oddly hypnotic eyes fixing on her intently. He took her by the arms and in a faintly surprised tone said, "I declare! You're trembling!"

"Am I?" she asked, trying to conceal the nervousness in her voice.

"Yes," he said in his precise way, his eyes not leaving her. "I think I know what's wrong!"

"What do you mean?"

"When I left with my father Angelica talked to you."

"Of course we talked," she said, trying to pretend that nothing out of the way had been discussed.

He frowned slightly. "You know what I mean!"

"Please, Terry," she said, "don't hold my arms so tightly! You are hurting me!"

He relaxed his grip of her a little and said, "I can quote what she told you. She talked about Ruth, didn't she? She told you that Ruth was murdered?"

She nodded. "Yes."

"And that it is the belief she was murdered by Jack the Ripper, did she tell you that as well?"

In a small voice, she again said, "Yes."

Disgust showed on her handsome husband's face. "So all my tact in keeping it from you has gone for nothing. All my effort to spare you this fearful knowledge has been wrecked in the matter of a few minutes."

"You mustn't be angry about it!" she protested.

Terence let her go almost roughly and turned to stare out the window in anger. "I did not want your arrival here marred by this grim news. I have tried to cancel it from my mind and I wanted you to be ignorant of it."

"That was almost too much to hope for," she said. "Especially with a new Jack the Ripper murder just committed. I would be bound to hear from someone!"

He turned to her again, his handsome face pale. "Then I would have hoped to be the one to tell you, myself."

"It is nothing to make such a fuss about," Susan protested. "Naturally I'm a little upset but I'll get over it. Best for me to find out at once."

"Angelica would be bound to tell you," he said in the same annoyed tone. "She hated Ruth because I married her."

"Did she, really?"

"Yes," he said, his sharp, black eyes searching hers. "I'm sure she also must have let you know the details of that. That I jilted her to marry Ruth."

Susan said, "She told me you had courted her until you

met Ruth. Then she and your brother began seeing each other and decided to marry."

"After I had married Ruth," he said. "I suppose I am wrong to attempt living in the same house with Phillip and her. But my father wished it and I have tried to obey his wishes even though he is no longer mentally competent at all times."

She said, "Pray do not distress yourself, I'm sure that I can get along with Angelica. And perhaps all the better for her being so frank in telling me about the situation here."

"I'm not sure her frankness was intended to be kind."

"No matter," she said. "I shall benefit by it."

"I had hoped she would be a good wife to my brother," Terence went on. "And to a degree she is. But she has a cold, revengeful nature and I have the conviction she has never forgiven me for spurning her for Ruth."

"She surely can't have the same feeling toward me," Susan pointed out. "I'm an innocent party. And she has a husband now."

"True," he said, rather unhappily. "What other scandalous details did she tell you?"

Susan spread her hands. "Very few. I do remember her saying that a medical student living here was questioned by the police."

"We were all questioned," he said with his handsome face bitter. "It was a loathsome business."

"I'm certain of that. You would be in no mood for it while you were still grieving for Ruth. She claimed that the police suspected this student and that later he left here and committed suicide."

Terence nodded. "That is correct. When I left for America I was under the impression that he had been Jack the Ripper. That there would be no more murders."

"And the news of the new one this morning came as an upset to you," she suggested.

"It did."

"Still, the authorities may be wrong," she said. "It is possible last night's murder was done by someone else. That they merely imitated the method of this Jack the Ripper."

Her husband's handsome face brightened. "I had never thought of that. You could be right."

"In any case," she said, "I would not worry so about it until more details are announced."

Terence showed all his Byronic charm at this moment. He came to her and gently took her in his arms and kissed her with deep affection.

"I knew I had found a proper wife in you," he told her. "And each day you make me more certain of it. Thank you for your understanding."

She smiled up at him. "It is my sincere wish to be a good wife to you."

"And I a good husband to you," Terence said. He sighed. "Please forgive my earlier show of anger. I cannot find it easy to forgive Angelica for tattling as she did, but perhaps in the long run, it will have been for the best."

"I'm positive of that."

"My illness has left me easy to upset," he explained. "My nerves have never properly recovered."

"And you did not get your proper rest last night," she said with sympathy. "You naturally don't feel well today. You must consider your health and avoid such night calls in future."

Her doctor husband looked uneasy at this. He said, "I would prefer that you put last night out of your mind."

"If you wish," she said.

He smiled rather wearily. "I must go visit the hospital

now. In the meantime you can busy yourself unpacking. I shall return in time for dinner."

"Very well," she said.

"At least you know the worst about this old house and the people in it," he sighed. "You mustn't allow Ruth's fate to depress you. Try and think of what happened as something apart from you."

"I shall," Susan promised.

"How do you feel about my father? Did he frighten you?"

"No," she said. "I'm sure he must have been a brilliant man in his day."

"He was," her husband agreed. "But only the ruins remain now. It is very sad! Very sad!"

He then left her and she began unpacking. She worked alone for a time, wanting to try and sort out her thoughts. Her husband had plainly shown his dismay and anger at her learning about his first wife's fate but she felt she shouldn't make too much of this. He had concealed these facts from her but he'd had good reasons for doing so. At least she now knew the truth and because of that felt she would be better able to understand him.

The physical collapse he'd mentioned must have come after the murder of his wife. And not much wonder! It was also easy to understand that he'd not yet completely recovered. That was why he'd become so quickly angered by Angelica's revelations. But with the passing of time surely his nerves would improve.

Her thoughts were shadowed by the events of the previous night. She still worried about his mysterious absence. It was quite possible that he'd told her the truth about being called to the bedside of a dying patient by his colleague, Dr. Donald Farrow. But the incident worried her. Especially since another Jack the Ripper murder had been committed during the night. The first in months, in fact the first since her husband's absence from and return to England!

She stood very still gazing into space as an expression of incredulity spread across her pretty face. How could she doubt this man who loved her and whom she loved, to this extent? It was terribly wrong of her to even allow herself to think that he might be somehow involved in the Jack the Ripper murders. It was not only disloyal on her part, it was stupid. She must put such thoughts out of her mind.

Having come to this wifely decision she pulled the bell cord to summon the maid to assist her with the balance of the unpacking. The yellow-haired Sally appeared almost at once and proved herself an excellent worker. With her help Susan completed the tedious task of unpacking the trunks in a relatively short time. The girl also liked to talk.

Susan asked her, "Have you been in service here long?"

"No, madam," the girl said. "But my aunt worked for the Ward family all her life and before she died she found me a post here."

"Do you like it?"

The girl hesitated over this. "Yes and no, madam. I was brought up in a small village and I miss it and all my friends. But Miss Samantha is very kind to everyone. Though some feel it isn't a good place to work."

Susan was puzzled. "Why do they say that?"

The girl with the yellow pigtails appeared uncomfortable. Then, in a confidential tone, she said, "I guess it's because of the ghost, madam."

"The ghost?"

"Yes. They do say Willowgate is haunted."

The girl's solemn words sent a slight chill running down Susan's spine. She said, "Go on. What sort of ghost?"

Sally looked embarrassed. "The first wife of the doctor's,

madam. The one what was murdered!"

"Oh!"

Sally nodded. "Yes, madam. There are those who claim they've seen her moving about the house in her shroud. And it is certain bad luck to see her, so they say."

"I'm sure that's ridiculous, superstitious talk," Susan said. "Have you ever seen the ghost?"

"No, madam," the girl admitted.

"Then I wouldn't believe that it exists until you do," she told her.

"No, madam," the girl said without much conviction in her tone.

After she finished unpacking Susan lay down for a short rest. Then she washed and changed into a dress she felt suitable for her first dinner in her new home. She was standing before the dresser mirror finishing with her hair when the door to the bedroom slowly creaked open, giving her a start.

She quickly turned to discover that the gaunt Samantha Ward had entered the room. The older sister of Terry's was dressed in another black dress and looking far more aged than she really was.

Susan said, "How are you, Samantha?"

The spinster looked distressed. "Did I frighten you?"

"Only because I didn't know who it was."

"I'm sorry," she said. And then her pinched face took on an admiring expression. "My! How nice you look!"

"Thank you," Susan said.

"I'm so happy that Terence found himself a wife like you," the thin woman said. "I never fully approved of Ruth, you know."

"Oh?"

Samantha looked grimly disapproving. "She was too demanding of my brother. She thought only of herself and of

56

her beauty. In the end she died because of that beauty. Jack the Ripper sought her out."

"So I've heard," she said.

"You are not vain as she was," the older woman went on. "I can tell. And vanity is the worst of sins, I always say."

Susan said, "I saw Ruth's portrait downstairs. She was truly a beautiful woman. I could never hope to match her."

"No need for you to," Samantha declared. "In any case you are pretty enough." She paused. "From all I've heard she wasn't so beautiful after that murderer finished carving her up."

"Dreadful!" Susan said, repulsed by the thought.

A grim smile played about the older woman's thin lips. "I call it justice. She got what she deserved. She was a flirt and she made life very difficult for my brother. But then both my brothers married the wrong women. You've met Angelica?"

"Yes."

"Then you must know she's a cold, despicable person. When she couldn't snare Terence she settled for Phillip. It is no wonder poor Phillip drinks."

This was news to Susan. She was learning a good deal about the family indirectly. She said, "I haven't yet met Phillip."

"You will," Samantha said. "He'll be here for dinner. I won't promise his condition but he'll be here."

She said, "What about young Dr. Oliver Rush?"

"He may be here and he may not," Samantha said. "It depends on how busy he is at the hospital."

"Perhaps he and my husband will come home together," she suggested.

"Maybe," the thin woman said. "I hope you remain here."

"I plan to," she replied, somewhat surprised. "After all it is my husband's home."

"And yours," Samantha said. "Don't forget that! Don't let her scare you away!"

She raised her eyebrows. "You mean Angelica?"

There was a slight pause as the older woman stood there facing her in the soft glow of the lamplit room. Samantha shook her head slowly. "No," she said. "Ruth."

"Ruth?" she echoed incredulously.

"Her ghost. It's been seen here," the older woman assured her.

Susan hardly knew what to reply. It was one thing to discuss such a thing with a teen-age servant girl but to talk about it with this woman was another matter. She pretended lack of knowledge, asking, "What do you mean?"

The thin woman's pinched face took on a gloating expression. She said, "I've seen her in her shroud! Not much beauty left now I can promise you! I stood in a cranny in the upper hall and watched her move by. You could see her white, decaying face beneath the shroud veils!"

She listened to the older woman's description of the ghost with a feeling of horror. Samantha Ward was actually glorying in Ruth's murder and her supposedly ghostly appearance. It was a macabre, unhealthy performance which made her doubt the sanity of the thin woman. Samantha's life of devotion to her aged father and her jealousy of her brothers had apparently warped her mind.

Swallowing hard she said, "I'm afraid I have no belief in ghosts."

Samantha's smile was knowing. "You will have before you've spent too many nights at Willowgate," was her warning. "You mark my words!"

The thin woman then left her to consider all this. Susan was shocked. Samantha's subtle madness was far more upsetting than old Simon Ward's senile dementia. Susan was left with the feeling that despite her air of friendliness the gaunt Samantha might actually hate her just as she'd hated Ruth. She would find this out in due time.

After a little she went downstairs. She'd hoped that Terry would have returned but there was no sign of him yet. She made her way to the drawing room, where she heard voices. Entering the big room with its gas-lit chandeliers bathing it in a soft glow she found Angelica, Samantha, and a stout, florid-faced man who she guessed must be Phillip Ward.

The stout man saw her and came forward with a smile on his rather porcine face. He had hair that was graying and stood up stiffly and a heavy gray mustache. There was no resemblance to her handsome husband in that bloated face.

"You are Susan!" he said warmly. "I am your brother-in-law, Phillip!"

"I'm glad to know you, Phillip," she said.

He bent forward and kissed her on the cheek and she was at once aware of a strong odor of whiskey about him. He chuckled and said, "Privilege of a member of the family, you know!"

Angelica had been watching all this with cold demeanor. Now she said, "You might show less ardor and offer Susan some sort of refreshment."

"Right this minute!" Phillip said with a wink of a bleary blue eye for Susan. "What would you like, my dear?"

"A taste of sherry would be very welcome," she said.

"Right!" her new brother-in-law said, going to the sideboard. "I like something a bit stronger myself. But I say sherry is all right in its place."

"It's too bad you don't drink it instead of filling yourself with whiskey," his wife said with an open show of disgust.

Samantha's thin face registered disapproval of this and she

turned to Susan to say, "I wonder where Terence is? He ought to be here for dinner. I've invited Dr. Farrow."

"Dr. Farrow," Susan said. "He's a neighbor, isn't he?"

"Yes. And a good friend of the family," Samantha told her.

Phillip Ward came to her with a glass of sherry. "There you are," he said.

She thanked him and took a sip of the wine. She was also worried about her husband and hoped he wasn't about to indulge in another of his disappearances.

To make conversation she turned to the stout Phillip, who was gulping down still another whiskey. She said, "I understand you are in the medical supply business."

"The only role for a frustrated doctor, my dear," the stout man said with a smile on his bloated face. "I thus share in a small way in the practice of the healing art.

"I should think it would be most interesting," she said.

As she spoke a tall, slim, red-haired young man in a gray suit which didn't fit too well came into the drawing room. He was good-looking in a boyish way, although there was little character in his face as yet. He smiled at her shyly as he waited to be introduced.

Phillip said, "May I present Dr. Oliver Rush, who is working at the hospital with Terence and living with us. Oliver, this is Mrs. Ward."

The young man extended a thin hand. "How do you do, Mrs. Ward. I have looked forward to meeting you."

"Well done!" the whiskey-happy Phillip commended him with a pat on the arm. "Keep that up, boy, and you'll have all the ladies of London at your feet!"

The young doctor blushed and told Susan, "I hope you are going to like England."

"I think I shall," she said. "Have you seen my husband?

He told me he was going to the hospital but he hasn't returned as yet."

The young man looked surprised. "I did see him in one of the wards about two hours ago but not afterward. I assumed he had come home."

"Not as yet," she said. "I guess something must have detained him."

"Yes, that must be it," Dr. Rush agreed, though he seemed puzzled by Terence's absence.

The young doctor moved on to join Angelica, who gave him a warm smile of greeting. The two began to talk in animated fashion and it seemed reasonably clear that Angelica enjoyed the attentions of the doctor. Susan saw that Phillip Ward was watching the two with a rather malicious look. Samantha had seated herself and seemed disinterested in conversing with anyone.

Hoping to relieve the strained situation Susan addressed herself to Phillip and said, "Does your father ever join you at the dinner hour?"

The stout man shook his head. "Hardly ever! There was a time . . . but not lately. His mind is clouded most of the time. He has a few periods of clarity and then he goes off into a blank spell. We've found it better to discourage him from joining us."

"That is sad," she said.

"The ravages of time," Phillip concluded and drained his glass.

Before she could make any reply to this a new face joined the group. From the hallway there appeared an aristocratic man with thinning gray hair and a stern countenance. He bore himself with the assurance of one who had long known a post of importance. Phillip at once went to him and brought him over to her.

"My dear," Phillip said, "I want you to meet one of your husband's colleagues and dearest friends, Dr. Donald Farrow."

She smiled at the newcomer. "I'm delighted to meet you. I've heard so much about you."

"And I about you," Dr. Farrow said, with a courtly bow and a stiff smile. "Terence wrote me at length about you from America."

"And so we meet at last," she said. "I'm only sorry that my husband isn't here yet. He went to the hospital and for some reason seems to have been delayed there."

Dr. Farrow nodded. "He has been away a long while. Possibly he had some matters to straighten away. I wouldn't worry about him, Mrs. Ward."

"Thank you," she said.

Samantha rose from her chair. "We'll wait five minutes more and if he hasn't arrived by then we must go in to dinner. Otherwise the roast beef will be ruined."

"Time for a final drink," Phillip Ward said happily after helping Dr. Farrow to one.

Susan found herself standing a distance from the others with the distinguished-looking doctor. She had heard he was a bachelor and judged that he must be at least twenty years older than her husband.

She said, "You and Terence have been together at the hospital for some time?"

He showed one of his stern smiles. "Yes. You might call us a team. I'm delighted that he has returned from America."

"And you lost no time in getting in touch with him, did you?" she said with a smile. "Was he able to help your patient last night?"

Dr. Farrow looked slightly bewildered. "Last night?"

"Yes," she said. "When you came and got him at the hotel.

I awoke later and was truly frightened. I had no idea where he might have gone. Later he explained that you had come for him."

The distinguished Dr. Farrow frowned. "My dear Mrs. Ward, I fear you must be making some error."

"Error?"

"Yes," he said. "I certainly didn't see your husband last night. Actually I missed him at the hospital this afternoon. So we haven't met yet."

Susan stood there staring at him with a shocked expression on her lovely face and fear seeping through her.

Chapter Four

Dr. Farrow at once said, "Is there anything wrong, Mrs. Ward?"

She shook her head. "No! No, it's quite all right. I was surprised for a moment. I was sure my husband mentioned your name but it must have been some other doctor."

The gray-haired man seemed disconcerted. "Surely it must have been. I didn't mean to upset you."

"Of course you didn't," she said. But she was fighting a battle to pretend to be calm. Her heart was pounding furiously and she feared she might faint.

The situation was saved by Phillip Ward coming over with his whiskey glass in hand and joining them. It gave her a chance to remain silent for a little and try and collect her wits. If Terry had lied to her about last night, and it seemed certain that he had, where had he been? What had he been doing on this night when the latest Jack the Ripper murder had been committed?

Phillip was asking the doctor, "What do you make of this latest killing? We all thought that young student who killed himself was Jack the Ripper. Now there is a new murder the police claim is the Ripper's work. Does that mean we were wrong?"

"I never agreed with the theory that the young doctor who boarded here was the criminal," Dr. Farrow said. "And it seems to me this vindicates him. The real Jack the Ripper is still at large."

"Then why did that fellow kill himself?" Phillip asked.

"That is another matter entirely," the doctor said sternly. "I'm satisfied as to his reasons but as a fellow doctor I'm unable to discuss them."

"Ah!" Phillip Ward said rather drunkenly and touched a forefinger to the side of his nose in a conspiratorial manner. "Professional ethics!"

"Whatever you like," Dr. Farrow said brusquely. "I don't wish to say anything more about it at the moment."

Samantha said, "I don't think we should discuss those awful murders at all. There has been far too much talk about them!"

Susan was still standing there trying to maintain a calm. All at once she heard the front door open and her husband's voice in the hall as he exchanged a greeting with Baker. And a moment later he advanced into the drawing room with his usual charm. She thought he had never looked more handsome.

"Greetings all!" he said. "My apologies for being late. My hansom cab lost a wheel on a bad piece of road and I had to find another. It delayed me a full half-hour." He came straight to her and kissed her on the cheek. "My special apologies to you, my dear."

"As long as you're here now," she said in a small voice.

"Let us go in to dinner at once," Samantha said. "I expect it is partly ruined by now."

They all crossed to the dining room on the other side of the house and took their places at a long table gleaming with fine china and silver on a spotless white linen tablecloth. Samantha presided at one end of the table and Terence at the other, with Susan on his right and Angelica on his left. The young Dr. Rush sat next to her and Dr. Farrow sat beside Susan. Phillip had the chair nearest his sister.

The dinner, contrary to Samantha's expectations, had not

been ruined by the long wait. The food was delicious and augmented by several fine wines. Susan tried to enter into the spirit of the occasion as best she could but found it difficult in her troubled state.

Terence must have noticed this as he asked her quietly, "Don't you feel well, darling? You're unusually quiet for you."

"I do have a slight headache," she said. "But perhaps it will pass."

"I surely hope so," her husband said as he turned to start a new discussion with Angelica.

At last dinner came to an end and they all moved back into the drawing room for coffee and brandy. She again found herself in the company of Dr. Farrow.

The tall, aristocratic-looking man glanced around to make sure they wouldn't be overheard by the others before he said, "I would like to have a short private talk with you, Mrs. Ward."

She stared up at him with troubled eyes. "What about?"

"I'd prefer not to say at the moment," he told her. "But I'd like to meet you tomorrow. It is my custom to take a stroll on the grounds of my estate before returning to the hospital in the afternoon. A bit of outdoor exercise for my health. I wonder if you might meet me and join me in my walk."

"Yes. I'd be quite willing to do that," she said. "What time?"

"Usually at two sharp," Dr. Farrow said. "In the event of rain I go straight back to the hospital. Mist and fog don't stop me. So you'll know by the weather."

"I'll go over to your place at two unless it is raining," she promised.

Dr. Farrow reached in his vest pocket and produced a large gold watch with Roman characters on its face. He studied the watch and said, "I must go now. I have to operate early in the morning and I count on a good night's sleep."

"Very well," she said. "I won't forget tomorrow."

"Excellent," the stern-faced doctor said. He next went to Samantha and thanked her for the dinner and said goodnight to the others, including Terence.

Terence saw him out and then returned to Susan. He smiled and asked, "How do you like him?"

"He's very nice," she said. "I can understand why you so admire him."

"I have enjoyed working with him," her husband agreed.

She said, "You must to leave your bed in the middle of the night to help him on a case."

Her husband showed slight embarrassment. "That was of no importance, really. I wish you'd just forget all about it."

Susan pretended surprise. "But I see it as an utter dedication to your profession!"

Terence sighed. "I don't want old Farrow to feel obligated to me. So I'd prefer that you said nothing of it to him or the others."

"If that's your wish," she replied quietly. She did not feel she had to let him know that she'd already questioned the doctor about the midnight incident and he'd seemed to know nothing about it.

"You look weary," her husband said solicitously. "I think you should go straight up to bed. I've a few papers to go over in my study but I'll join you very shortly."

She saw that all the others had vanished, probably to their own rooms. She gave her husband a worried look. "You shouldn't stay up too late either. You have been under more strain than me and you're only now recovering from your illness."

Starting to escort her to the foot of the stairway, he said,

"I'll be all right. And I won't take long with the papers. I ought to be upstairs in twenty minutes or so." He kissed her good-night and stood at the bottom of the stairway until she'd reached the landing.

She made her way down the dark hallway to the door of their apartment with her being shaken by misgivings. She knew that her husband had lied to her but she wasn't positive why. Dr. Farrow had gone out of his way to advise her that he wished to speak with her and she felt this could only mean he had some warning for her. Warning about what? Could it have to do with Jack the Ripper, the monstrous criminal whose crimes had been resumed with the return of her husband to England. Could that mean that he knew more about the murders than he wanted to let on?

These questions and others like them continued to plague her as she entered the parlor of the apartment. Sally had been there and had placed a single lamp on one of the parlor tables and another in the bedroom on the bedside table. They gave off light without making either room bright. Her nerves were on edge as a result of the events of the night. Slowly she began to undress and prepare for bed.

She was in her nightgown sitting at the dresser mirror brushing her long brown hair when suddenly reflected in the mirror there was a veiled, wraithlike figure. The figure stood in the doorway between the bedroom and parlor. A shadowy gray phantom standing there in the distance studying her. She screamed out her fear and in the same instant the macabre figure vanished. Susan jumped to her feet and stood leaning against the dresser staring at the doorway, expecting the ghost to reappear.

But it didn't. Instead her husband was next framed in the doorway. He said, "I heard you scream as I came in. What's the matter?"

She hurried across the room to his arms. Looking up at him frantically, she exclaimed, "Didn't you see her?"

"Her?" he sounded and looked puzzled.

"The ghost! The figure in the gray shroud!"

He stared at her. "You can't be serious!"

"But I am," she insisted, on the verge of tears. "I saw her just now. Standing just about where you are."

He was holding her in his arms and now he gazed down at her and said, "I suspect someone has been telling you stories."

"Why?"

"To make you have such fancies," he said. "I know what some of those in this house are saying. They are telling that Ruth's ghost returns here."

"Yes," she said tautly.

"It's all nonsense," he assured her. "Just the imaginings of the superstitious. It started because Ruth was so brutally slain. But can you imagine her spirit returning here? Why should it?"

She insisted, "I know that I saw something."

"A shadow," he said. "A shadow on the wall that set your nerves to work."

She made no reply to this. But she did not believe his too simple explanation. She knew that she had seen a definite figure. The memory of its horror was etched in her mind. But he did not want to accept this and at this point she was too weary and confused to argue.

They went to bed. She fell asleep from sheer exhaustion and slept on until she was wakened by weird howlings from somewhere in the house. They quickly brought her out of her sound sleep to lean on an elbow in the bed.

"Terry!" she cried and at the same time shook the shoulder of her sleeping husband.

"What's that?" he mumbled sleepily and also sat up partially.

"Listen!" she said, staring into the darkness in terror.

The eerie scream came again and then faded into silence.

"It's nothing," her husband assured her. "You're hearing my father cry out! He has nightmares and screams like that. It is unpleasant but hardly frightening when you recognize the cries for what they are. The torments of a sick old man."

"You are sure?" she said.

"Of course I am," he said, rather testily. "Now please go to sleep again."

She lay back on her pillow with the echo of the terrifying screams still in her ears. She knew her husband's story could be correct but she was still worried. She waited for the cries to come again and fell asleep a second time waiting for them.

When she awoke in the morning her husband had already risen and left for the hospital. After she dressed she went to the window and saw that the fog had lifted a little but it was still a gray day. She prayed there would be no rain as she wanted to keep her appointment with the doctor, who lived next door.

Angelica was her companion at the breakfast table and she asked her how to get to the doctor's grounds. She said, "I had an invitation to see his house."

The blond girl raised an eyebrow. "That's interesting. He rarely invites anyone over there. He must have taken a liking to you."

"I didn't realize that," she said.

"It doesn't matter," Angelica told her. "The quickest way is across our front lawn to the row of willow trees and the hedge beyond. You'll find a passage cut through the hedge and it joins his grounds with ours."

"Thank you," Susan said. "If it rains I'll go another day."

"You'll probably find the house interesting," Angelica said. "The style is nice and it is older than ours. If you meet his sister you may find her a trifle eccentric. She never leaves the house."

"Why?"

"She has a fear of people," the blond girl informed her. "I suppose she is a little mad. But she never entertains more than one person at a time and she has only a small staff to operate that big house."

"That must make it difficult for Dr. Farrow," she said.

"He has no social life as a result," Angelica agreed. "But he doesn't seem to mind. To be truthful, in spite of his dignified façade, I'd call him somewhat eccentric himself."

"Why do you say that?"

"His refusal to make his sister behave normally and his devotion to her. There can be no other reason for his bachelorhood."

"But there's nothing so wrong in that," she protested.

"Perhaps you don't think so," Angelica said in her cold way, "but I do."

As soon as breakfast was over she left the blond young woman. She did not care for Angelica or agree with her point of view. Further, she was almost certain that this sister-in-law of hers was carrying on a flirtation with young Dr. Oliver Rush. And judging by the ugly expression on Phillip's face as he'd watched them he was not unaware of what was going on either.

She moved down one of the long dark corridors again feeling the grim oppressiveness of the old mansion. She was still worried about her husband's behavior and convinced that she had seen a ghost! The screams had also been terrifying to her. All in all she was finding Willowgate a decidedly unpleasant place and she was anxious to find out what Dr.

Donald Farrow wished to confide in her. She was almost certain it was a warning.

Suddenly she was confronted by what she could only imagine to be some supernatural figure. A dark clad, black-faced man in a battered top hat came to a halt directly before her. She gave a small cry of dismay.

To her surprise the specter politely doffed his hat to reveal a thick head of black-matted hair and said, "Beggin' your pardon, miss, I'm Flagg, the chimney sweep. I've a couple of my lads at work here today."

"Chimney sweep?" she said with some relief.

"That's right, miss. You can always depend on Flagg," the weird figure said, his hat still in hand. "If you'll excuse me now I'm expectin' one of my boys to be coming down the dining room chimney at any moment." And with a quick bow he hurried off.

Susan stood there watching him vanish and feeling more than a little ashamed that she'd allowed herself to be frightened by so ordinary a person. It served to warn her that she might be allowing her imaginings to get the better of her in other instances. She blamed her edginess on the old mansion with its foreboding air.

She went on to the dining room in time to see the chimney sweep's lad appear in the fireplace where the sweep was waiting for him. The boy seemed no more than seven or eight years old and he was black with soot. As the sweep instructed him on what he should do next Susan watched and felt that it was a miserable occupation for any lad of that age. It was no wonder that the child looked ill and undernourished.

The day continued to be fair although there was no sun. The fog lifted almost completely by the time she left the house to meet Dr. Farrow. She followed the instructions which she'd obtained from Angelica and soon found the section cut through the hedge. She went on to the adjoining grounds and saw the splendid Tudor style house and Dr. Donald Farrow standing by its door. As soon as he spied her he waved and came to meet her.

"Good afternoon, Mrs. Ward," the stern-faced man said as they met in the center of the lawn.

"I wanted to be on time," she told him.

"You are," he assured her. He was wearing a long-tailed black coat and gray trousers and a black top hat. "Shall we stroll while we talk?"

"By all means."

"I find the exercise most beneficial," the man at her side said.

"You have lovely grounds," Susan said. "It would be a shame not to enjoy them."

A slight shadow crossed his face. "I regret that my sister doesn't take advantage of them. She suffers from a strange reticence and has no desire to leave the house or meet anyone. As a result we live an extremely quiet life. My only social activity is with your husband's family."

"That is too bad," she said.

"It is," he sighed. "That is why I suggested that we meet out here and have a stroll while we talked."

"I think it's an excellent idea," she told him.

They had reached a barrier of bushes so they turned and began walking back toward the dark Tudor mansion in which Dr. Farrow and his sister lived.

He cleared his throat and said, "I'm most anxious to be your friend, Mrs. Ward. Just as I am your husband's friend."

"I feel that strongly," she said. "And I'm grateful."

The gray-haired doctor gave her a questioning look. "How do you find Willowgate?"

"Frightening," she said frankly.

"I was sure you must," he said. "In the old days when your husband's father was himself it was quite different. Things have changed with his failing mental state. And of course Phillip's drunkenness is also a problem."

"I've sensed that," she said.

"No one really heads the household now," Dr. Farrow said. "Samantha acts as a sort of housekeeper but she has no real authority. Terence was on his way to taking over when the tragedy of Ruth's murder overtook him. After that he fell to pieces. I'm trusting that his marriage to you will give him a new lease on life."

"I hope I may be able to help him," she said seriously. "But there are times when I find him very strange."

"I'm not surprised," the gray-haired doctor said.

She hesitated and then told him, "I began to feel a certain uneasiness after our marriage, when we were in New York waiting for the sailing which brought us here. Several times he left me for long intervals without any really solid excuse. And then on our first night in London he vanished in the night and on his return told me that you had called him out to see a patient. Last night you denied this."

The stern man halted and faced her. "I regret that I had to dispute Terence's story."

"Then he lied to me," she said unhappily.

"In a sense, yes," he agreed.

"And it was on that night the Jack the Ripper murders began once again," she said in a taut voice.

"I realize that."

She gave him a frightened look. "I know you have asked me here to reveal something to me. Has it to do with my husband and those dreadful murders?"

Dr. Farrow frowned. "Not directly. You know that Ruth

was thought to have been murdered by the Ripper."

"Yes."

"There were two other similar murders in this area, both said to bear Jack the Ripper's trademark of surgical mutilation. So most of us have been questioned by the police. Including Terence."

"Go on," she said.

He sighed and stared out across the lawn. It was plainly difficult for him to proceed. "I know that you are new here and a great deal of this must be terrifying for you. But I feel I must explain the likely reason for your husband's mysterious behavior."

She gazed up into the stern face of the top-hatted man fearful of what he might be about to tell her. In the distance a bird flew out of the trees and soared high in the air uttering a mournful cry. The bleak day was exactly right for dark revelations.

Dr. Farrow said sadly, "In a sense your husband has fallen a victim to medicine. His total dedication to the surgeon's art has led him into dire circumstances."

"Please continue."

"This goes back to 1884," the gray-haired doctor said. "It was in that year we learned of a new anesthetic extracted from South American cocoa leaves. Sigmund Freud showed a particular interest in its possibilities. This anesthesia was very valuable for local use. It could be injected into the tissues around a nerve and provide a quick regional blockage. Your husband was one of the first surgeons in England to make full use of the drug."

Susan was listening with great interest. "And?"

"In 1885 your husband published a paper on this anesthesia which was lauded in medical circles. He and two of his young assistants did many experiments with the drug. One of his assistants was the young doctor residing at Willowgate who later took his own life."

"Of course. I've heard about him."

The stern face of Dr. Farrow was shadowed. "The name of this anesthetic was cocaine. And your husband found that by sniffing small quantities his mental powers were heightened, his body needed less sleep, and his capacity for work became infinite. What he didn't know at the time was that cocaine was habit-forming."

She listened with growing dismay. "Then what?"

"I learned from Terence that not only he but both of his young assistants were taking the drug. They had been sniffing cocaine regularly and now the addiction stage had set in. They were becoming unstable and drifting into a dream world of fantasies."

Susan was shocked. "How horrible for them!"

"Indeed it was," Dr. Farrow said grimly. "Terence came to me for advice and I told him there was only one hope. To cure himself of the drug habit."

"And?"

"Then Ruth was murdered. I needn't go into detail about that. You have heard the story. It completely broke him mentally. He entered a hospital here and put himself under their control. His two assistants did not take this drastic step and their fates were tragic. One of them was run down by a dray and killed apparently while in a drugged state. The other moved from Willowgate and gave up medical practice. Some time later he hung himself in his lodgings."

She said, "But wasn't he supposed to be Jack the Ripper? I've heard that and also that he hung himself out of remorse."

The gray-haired doctor frowned. "I regard that story as quite unfounded. I think the Ripper murder the other night proves that the young man was not the guilty person."

"What of my husband?"

"I don't know. I must be frank. He may have reverted to the use of cocaine. That could account for his absences in New York and again in London. He may be taking only small amounts in his continuing struggle to shake the addiction or he may be fully addicted once more. Only time will reveal that."

"What can I do?" she asked in despair.

"There is not much to be done," the veteran doctor admitted in a worried tone. "Terence should not have married you without revealing all his background. I think that most unfair."

"So my husband is a drug addict."

"He may have overcome his addiction or he may be actively battling it," Dr. Farrow said, "but judging by what you've told me he is behaving in an abnormal manner. That is surely not a good sign."

"This happened to him before Ruth was murdered?"

"Definitely," the doctor said. "And when the murder took place I'm certain the police eyed Terence with some suspicion."

"With suspicion?" she was further shocked.

He nodded. "Yes. He wasn't able to conceal that he'd been on drugs. I believe that for a time they held a theory that he might have committed the Jack the Ripper murders while under the evil influence of cocaine. The murders were done by one possessing medical knowledge and it is possible his mind was twisted by cocaine."

"You don't really think Terence a mad murderer?" she asked in a stunned way.

"No," he said. "But I have been worried about it. And the fact there were no murders when he was out of the country and they began so soon after his return makes me worry even more. Plus the fact that he was absent without explanation in the middle of the night when this latest crime was committed."

Her eyes were wide with the staggering fear the doctor's words brought her. She gasped, "No, not Terence! Not my husband!"

"I think not and I hope not," the gray-haired doctor said. "But I felt you must be told the facts."

"I was frightened before," she told him, "and now I'm filled with despair and terror."

"You mustn't give way to your feelings," Dr. Farrow said. "We must both try to help Terence and prove that he had no part in the murders. I firmly believe he is innocent despite the circumstantial evidence pointing to him and the suspicions of the police."

"He hasn't been the person I first met for some weeks," she worried.

"I'd put that down to increasing strain and a possible reversion to cocaine," the doctor said. "If he is back on the drug again his condition will grow gradually more unstable and we'll know."

"And in the meantime?"

"Carry on as best you can."

"It won't be easy."

"I realize that," the veteran doctor said. "But it is for the man you love."

She gave him a despairing look. "I'm beginning to wonder if the man I loved ever truly existed or if I deluded myself and fell in love with a façade of a man who bore no resemblance to the real person."

"Terence was a fine man," Dr. Farrow said. "God willing, he can be one again. Meanwhile we must have faith."

"I'm alone in a strange country," she said. "And there's no

one at the house to help."

"I realize that. But I shall help as best I can. That is why I sought you out for this talk. At least now you are aware of the problem."

"You think that it is best that I not let Terence be aware of my knowledge of his drug addiction?"

"I would say so at this time," the veteran doctor said. "It may be at some future moment it will be necessary for you to speak out. Now I would hold my silence if I were you."

"I shall try," she said.

Dr. Farrow asked her, "How are you and Angelica getting along?"

"She is very difficult."

"I would expect that," he said grimly. "Though she is married to Terence's brother she has never recovered from her infatuation for your husband. She is still jealous of him."

"I know."

"Yet she continues to flirt with that young Dr. Rush and any other man who will look at her," Dr. Farrow said bitterly. "She is a very mixed-up person. You must be wary of her."

"I know that," she said. "Samantha is odd but I like her much more."

"She means well," he agreed. "Now I suppose we must part. I have to return to the hospital and you to Willowgate. Please don't let your nervous state be worse because of what I've revealed to you. I have done this for your protection, not to hurt you."

"I understand," she said. "But I'm so afraid of drugs and what they can do."

"I have the feeling Terence has seen the worst of it. So you mustn't be too alarmed."

She was going to ask him about the ghost, the hideous shrouded figure she'd seen the night before but there wasn't time. They said a hasty good-bye and she returned to the grounds of Willowgate.

She walked back slowly to the great red-brick mansion still in a daze from what she'd heard. It presented so many new problems for her she wondered how she could continue on. She had only to appeal to her uncle Charles back in Philadelphia and he would welcome her home. Money was no difficulty. A considerable sum of her own fortune had been transferred to a London bank account.

The great problem was that she loved her husband. She did not want to desert Terence when he perhaps needed her most. But what if he were still a drug addict as Dr. Farrow suspected or even the murderous Jack the Ripper as the police had once thought? She refused to believe that either of these two things could be true. She had to keep faith in her husband!

This inward debate continued to bother her as she made her way up the dark stairway to her suite. When she reached her bedroom she found the maid, Sally, there. The girl with the yellow pigtails had seemingly been cleaning the room but at the moment Susan entered Sally was standing before a long mirror admiring herself in a crimson velveteen rain cape and cap which she'd taken from Susan's closet. It was Susan's favorite rainwear cloak.

The girl heard her enter and turned around with an air of guilt. "I'm sorry, madam!"

She decided not to be angry with the girl. After all it was a small offense. With a wry smile, she said, "Did you want to see whether crimson suited you, Sally?"

The girl hastily took off the cloak and cap. "I was taken by it, madam," she confessed. "And I gave way to the temptation of seeing if it suited me."

"No harm done," she said.

"Please don't tell Miss Samantha what I did," the girl said in a pleading tone.

"I have no intention of telling anyone," Susan assured her. "Put the cloak away and we'll forget all about it."

"Thank you, madam," the girl said gratefully.

As she watched the girl hang the cloak up in its closet again she felt a sudden sympathy for her. And as Sally turned around to leave the room Susan told her, "I'm certain I have some things I will be disposing of shortly. And since you are about the same size perhaps you would like them?"

A smile crossed the maid's face. "Would you be so kind, madam?"

"I promise I'll sort some things out at the first chance," she told her.

Sally went off with a happy air and Susan promised herself to check her wardrobe at the first opportunity. She knew there were some dresses she would not want again and it was evident that Sally would value them highly.

Crossing to the dresser she glanced down to find some hairpins when her eyes fixed on something she'd not seen there before. It lay on the dresser top directly in front of her, a bouquet of blue violets, artificial violets bound in pale green net and tied with a pale green ribbon.

Thinking that Terence might have left them for her as a surprise she lifted them and held them close to her nose. There was a faint fragrance of perfume from them mixed with another odor which she could not place at first. And then she decided that it must be a stale, mildewed smell. She was standing with the violets in her hand when in the reflection of the mirror she saw the gaunt Samantha enter the room behind her.

She turned, still holding the bouquet of artificial violets, to greet the older woman. "I was about to go downstairs," she said.

Samantha crossed the room to join her. She said, "I was up seeing my father for a little. He is not at all well today."

"That is too bad," Susan sympathized.

Suddenly the older woman's gaze became fixed on the violets she was holding in her hand. In a hushed voice, Samantha asked, "Where did you get them?"

"I found them on my dresser," she said. "Do you know anything about them?"

The gaunt Samantha raised her eyes to meet Susan's and she saw the look of true horror in them as the thin spinster told her, "Yes. Ruth was buried with that bouquet in her hands!"

Chapter Five

Susan was so shocked by the older woman's words that she almost dropped the bouquet. The strange, sickly perfume of the artificial flowers was explained. But what did it mean? How could they have come to rest on her dresser?

She said, "You must be wrong! They can't be the same flowers."

Samantha took the artificial bouquet from her and with an assured manner found the tail of one of the ribbons and held it out for her to read. "See!" she said.

Susan studied the crumpled ribbon and saw that the single word, "Ruth," had been neatly crocheted there. She said, "You say Ruth was buried with this in her hands?"

"Yes," the older woman said in a low voice. "Violets were her favorite flower. I made this bouquet myself and crocheted her name on the ribbon. Then I placed it in her hands as she lay in her coffin!"

"Someone must have taken it out before the coffin was closed."

"No," Samantha argued. "I was standing by the coffin when the lid was placed on it. The flowers were still in her hands then."

"But that's impossible! How could they get to my dresser top from the grave?"

The gaunt woman gave her a knowing glance. "You should be able to guess that. She brought them to you. I'd call it a sign! A message from the dead!"

"You can't believe that!" she protested.

"I must," she said, gazing down at the violets which she still held.

"It has to be a sick prank of someone's," she protested.

"No. You saw Ruth's name on it. These are the same flowers she held in those, cold, dead hands. I know. I placed them there."

"You're asking me to accept that Ruth's ghost brought them here?"

"Yes," the gaunt Samantha said solemnly. "We know that her phantom figure has been seen in the house."

She was about to offer a rebuttal when she recalled her own experience of the night before. Her pretty face became a mask of fear as she remembered that briefly seen shrouded head in the mirror. She'd been thoroughly shocked by the experience but her husband had insisted she'd seen nothing but a shadow. And she'd allowed him to persuade her this was so though she'd known better. Now it seemed she was being given proof that the ghostly figure of Ruth had been in her bedroom.

In a taut voice, she protested, "I don't know what to say."

"Best to accept the truth," Samantha declared, her thin, sallow face solemn.

"I must think about it," she faltered. "There has to be some explanation."

Samantha handed the violets back to her. "You take them. She wants you to have them."

Susan drew back. "No. I'd rather you kept them."

"I couldn't do that," Samantha told her. And she placed the violets on the dresser where Susan had found them in the first place. "I wouldn't dare interfere with her wishes."

"It's too fantastic!" Susan protested, but Samantha merely shrugged before she turned and left the room.

She stood there staring at the artificial bouquet for a

moment and not knowing what to do. Seized by an overwhelming desire not to have to see it she quickly opened an unused drawer at the bottom of one end of the dresser and thrust the bouquet in it. Then she slammed the drawer shut and stood there trembling.

After a little the physical shock wore off and she fixed her hair and went downstairs. In the drawing room she found Angelica reading. The blond girl put her book aside as Susan came in to join her.

"I've been reading Thackeray," the blond girl said. "He is one of my favorites." And then staring at her, she added, "You're so very pale! You look as if you'd seen a ghost!"

"Do I?" she said, sinking down in one of the antique chairs opposite her sister-in-law.

"And that would not be so out of the question in this house," Angelica went on to say. "Did you meet Dr. Farrow?"

"Yes."

"Your talk couldn't have been too pleasant to leave you looking so ill."

"It was all right."

"What do you really think of him?" Angelica asked, looking at her sharply.

She hesitated. "He seems very nice. Rather stiff in his manner but I'm sure he's a good friend of Terence's."

"He'd have you believe that anyway," the blond girl said maliciously.

Susan was surprised. "Don't you think he is?"

"I'm not sure."

"Why?"

Angelica seemed to be considering. Then she said, "For one thing, he's such a strange person. And his sister is even more odd."

"He mentioned that."

"Oliver Rush says that Dr. Farrow is not nearly as popular at the hospital as Terence even though he is his senior. The patients and the staff prefer Terence every time."

"Still, Dr. Farrow may be a very fine man."

Angelica smiled thinly. "He tries to give that impression."

"I'm inclined to accept it."

"I keep thinking of those Jack the Ripper murders," Angelica said. "The police at one time felt sure the killer lived within a few blocks of here. I wouldn't be surprised if they assigned someone to the area again."

"You honestly believe that?" she asked, alarmed for her husband.

"Why not? The murders have resumed."

"But why should Dr. Farrow be considered by the police?"

"Why not?" Angelica inquired airily. "He's peculiar enough in his own way and so is his sister." The blond girl leaned forward in a conspiratorial manner. "And don't forget he is an expert surgeon and so is the Ripper!"

Susan clasped the arms of her chair not knowing quite what to say. She had never considered this possibility before. She tried to see the stern Dr. Farrow in the role of a murderer and found it difficult. Yet the veteran surgeon had told her some damning things about Terence, perhaps wanting to seed doubts in her mind about him. Often murderers turned out to be people whom you least suspected. And Dr. Farrow could be one of this group.

Angelica was watching her with a kind of gloating triumph showing on her attractive face. "Well, what do you think?" she asked.

"I don't know what to think any more," she confessed unhappily. "I would like to believe that Dr. Farrow is my good friend."

"He surely pretends to be our friend but that means very little."

Susan said, "I thought that medical student who lived here and later killed himself might have been Jack the Ripper."

"John Morley!" Angelica said with something between anger and disappointment. "I can't think of a more unlikely murderer."

"You knew him well, then?" she suggested.

Angelica crimsoned. "He was a nice young man. I've tried to befriend all the young doctors who have lived here."

"I noticed you and Dr. Rush are good friends," Susan said pointedly.

Angelica's face was a positive crimson now. She said, "I live a very lonely life here. Phillip is a drunkard as you know. The little time when his mind is clear he devotes to his business. He doesn't show any love for me and so I must find companionship somewhere else."

"I see," she said quietly, amazed that the blonde should so willingly admit to her flirtations.

"You know what I think?" Angelica asked.

"What?"

"I think Jack the Ripper will strike again and again until he is caught. And when he is he'll turn out to be someone really well known."

"You mean someone really famous?"

"Yes," Angelica said. "Perhaps some titled person . . . a member of society. Remember, all his victims have been drawn from women of the lower classes."

"Except for Ruth," she said.

"Except for Ruth," Angelica agreed. "And that could have been purely an accident. He might have taken her for someone else."

"If he came from this area of London he should have

known her," she pointed out.

"When you're attacking someone in the dark, ready to commit a murder, how much time do you have to check an identity?" the blond girl suggested.

"That is true," she agreed.

Angelica rose and picked up her book. With her usual mocking manner she told her, "So I'd not pay too much attention to anything the doctor had to say. It's possible he may be merely protecting himself."

The blond woman left her alone in the drawing room even more confused than before. She sat for a fairly long while in the big chair thinking about it all and realizing that she was only more bewildered than she had been. After a little she rose from the chair and strolled slowly down the high-ceilinged drawing room to the fireplace and the full-length portrait above it. She stood staring up at the painting of the beautiful girl who had been her predecessor as Terence's wife. And she tried to picture her as the shrouded horror of a ghost which had presumably left the violet bouquet on her dresser.

She was still standing there in the shadowed room gazing up at the sad-eyed Ruth in the dark painting when she heard a stealthy footstep behind her. The sound made her wheel around in fear to see the ancient Dr. Simon Ward standing there.

The bearded old man said, "I know you. You are my son's new wife."

She saw that he was having one of his more rational moments and so felt less afraid of being alone with him.

She even managed a smile for him.

"That's right," she said. "I'm Terence's new wife. Can you remember my name?"

The old man hesitated, his eyes slightly squinted in

thought. Then he ventured, "Ruth?"

"No," she said, and pointed to the painting. "That is Ruth up there."

Dr. Simon Ward gazed up at the painting. "She was lovely too."

"Much more so than I could ever hope to be," she said.

The old man gave her a strange look. "But you are alive and she is dead. Dead and buried!"

"Yes. That is very sad."

The bearded old surgeon gazed at her intently. "Death is always sad in the young! In the old and mad like me it can be a blessing!"

"You shouldn't talk of death," she told him. "You seem very well today."

"I slipped away from Baker," the old man said with a sly chuckle. "He doesn't know I'm down here. They won't let me come down here any more."

"I think that is wrong," she said. "You should be free to come join us when you wish."

"You are right!" he agreed, firming back his shoulders. "I was a famous surgeon once. I helped found the hospital where Terence and Farrow work."

"I didn't know that," she said.

He made an impatient gesture. "No one remembers! I hoped to have two sons in surgery but Phillip proved a failure! He could not wield the lancet! He drew back from the cadaver! A weakling, and he bears the name of Ward!"

In an attempt to placate him, she said, "Not everyone is suited to medicine. He has done very well in his purveying of surgical instruments."

"He failed me," the old man said, with his eyes now showing a mad gleam. Staring at her, he demanded, "Are you one of the nurses that lady with the lamp has brought us?"

She was baffled by his sudden change of tone and manner. "If you're asking me if I'm a nurse, no I'm not!"

"Then what are you doing here, miss," he said, his bearded face angry. He pointed a forefinger at her. "We are waging a war here! This is a serious business! The casualties are mounting! I'm wanted at the field hospital!"

He had moved on to a ranting mood as he shouted the last words. The shouts brought Baker running into the room in an apologetic fashion.

Baker told her, "I'm sorry, madam. He got away while I was busy. I hope he hasn't bothered you!"

"It's all right," she said.

Baker spoke placatingly to the old man and managed to get him out of the room after a little. She could still hear their voices as they argued in mounting the stairs. She had almost managed a rational conversation with Dr. Simon Ward but in the end he'd wandered back to madness.

The peak moment of her day came when Dr. Terence Ward came home from the hospital earlier than usual and took her in his arms. For a moment she forgot all her other troubles. She truly loved Terence and only wanted to protect and help him.

He smiled down at her and said, "How did you spend the day?"

"I kept busy."

"Excellent," he said. "It is idleness which breeds unhappiness. And I have had a most active day at the hospital. I shall have to return there a little later in the evening but I made it a point to be home early."

"Must you return to the hospital tonight?"

"Imperative," he said. "I have patients who must be seen again before morning. But with luck I shan't be away long."

She stroked his arm. "I become so uneasy when you're not here."

"Why should you be?" he wanted to know. "You have all the others in the family to keep you company."

"You don't understand," she protested. "It is you that I miss."

He placed an arm around her as they started up the stairs. "I promise that once I get things in order at the hospital I'll give you a lot more of my time. During my absence things had become very mixed up. It isn't easy getting them in order again."

"I suppose not," she sighed.

Dinner was a fairly pleasant occasion principally because Terry seemed to be in one of his best moods. She was pleased by this and also a little concerned. Could his high spirits be the result of cocaine sniffed before his return home? She tried to dismiss this thought and enjoy the moment but the shadow lingered there in the back of her mind. Phillip, on the other hand, had managed to get a little more drunk than usual and was loud and talkative.

He announced, "Everyone who came in the store today had the name of Jack the Ripper on his lips."

Angelica raised her eyebrows. "Is there that much interest?"

"The Queen has written another letter to *The Times*," her husband informed her. "I hear that Scotland Yard are at their wit's end trying to find some clues to this latest murder."

Samantha said, "I do not think the Ripper is a proper subject for table conversation."

"Nor do I," Terence said, losing all his good humor. "I suggest you change the subject, brother."

Phillip eyed him with drunken bravado. "Why should I?

I'm not so much of a dolt that I don't know how to conduct a proper conversation!"

"We've had enough of Jack the Ripper," Terence said angrily.

Phillip ignored him and grinned at Susan. "Your husband is on the Ripper's side because the fellow happens to be handy with a scalpel."

Susan said, "Is there any new word about who the killer might be?"

"Absolutely none!" Phillip said with delight. "Maybe he's one of our fine doctors! They really enjoy cutting people up, you know. I didn't have any taste for it."

"Phillip!" Samantha said in an unusually stern tone. "We will have no more of such talk!"

Phillip picked up his wine glass. "All right," he said with a disgruntled air and took a big swig of wine.

It was a pleasant evening and she walked out with her husband as he made his way to the stable where the groom had a coach waiting for him. Terence was still in an annoyed mood about his brother's talk at the dinner table.

He mused, "I don't know why Phillip has to be such a boor!"

Her arm linked in his, she said, "I don't think he means to be."

"I wish I could feel the same way," he said. "All that needless talk about Jack the Ripper at the dinner table."

"In a way it had interest."

He stared at her in a shocked mood. "You mean to say you enjoyed it?"

"Not enjoyed it," she said. "But I do have interest in it. I think most everyone in London is following the case. Aren't you interested at all? Ruth is supposed to have died at his hands."

Terry frowned. "I have never believed that."

"No?"

"No. I told the police so when they came here questioning us. But you can't reason with them."

"Are they really so hardheaded?"

"I found them so in this," her husband said. "I was numbed by Ruth's murder or I would have handled them differently. In my view they did very little to solve the case."

"And now another woman has been murdered," she said.

"It will go on," he predicted with a sullen expression on his handsome, Byronic face. "I have every reason to think that. The fellow will continue until he is caught."

"Not a pleasant thought," she said as they reached the carriage.

"It is not," he said. "So I warn you to be careful. He was reputed to be active in this district."

"So I've heard," she said. "I shall certainly be on the alert."

Terry smiled at her. "I can't afford to lose you now," he said. He gave her a parting kiss and then got in the carriage. The coachman flicked his whip and the two gray horses started off. She watched the carriage vanish down Elgin Street. Because it was not yet dark she remained in the garden for a little. Twilight came and with it a kind of melancholy. The ending of day nearly always had this effect on her. A dog barked somewhere in the distance and night birds called out a mournful message that darkness was on its way. Soon the night things would take over!

She sat thinking about her husband and feeling more strongly than ever that he had conquered his drug habit and that he could never have been Jack the Ripper. She wanted to believe those things and so she tried to convince herself.

A male figure came slowly across the garden to the marble

bench where she was seated. As he drew nearer she saw that it was young Dr. Oliver Rush.

The young man stood before her and asked, "May I sit with you, Mrs. Ward?"

"If you like," she said in friendly fashion. "And since we are all living here together you may as well call me Susan and I shall use your name, Oliver."

The young man sat close to her and smiled. "That suits me very well, Susan."

"You weren't needed at the hospital tonight?" she said.

"No."

"My husband had to return."

The young doctor gazed at her in the growing shadows and said, "Will you be angry if I say something rather personal, Susan?"

She met his gaze. "No. I don't think so," she told him.

"About Dr. Ward returning to the hospital tonight," the young man said. "In my opinion it wasn't necessary."

"Oliver!" she reproached him. "How can you sat that? How can you be so disloyal to my husband?"

"Because I must speak frankly to you," was his earnest reply. "I want you to know the truth."

"It seems that everyone does," she suggested, "but I always find these truths are unpleasant."

"Mine will also be in that category," the young doctor said. "Before I left the hospital I heard Dr. Ward distinctly tell his assistant that he would not be returning there tonight."

She listened with growing dismay. "You overheard him say that?"

"I did," he said. "So I very well know that he cannot have gone there now."

"But where has he gone?" she wanted to know. "And why?"

The young man's face was now blurred by the shadows of the coming darkness. He said, "I can't imagine. But I do think he is being unfair to you. I can't bear to see him treating you in this fashion. You are so obviously true and loving."

She listened to his words and said, "And what is your interest?"

"I am your friend, Susan," he said, and reached out and took her hand in his. "I wish I could be even more than that but it seems the fates have played a cruel trick on us. You married him!"

She was astonished by this announcement of the young doctor. She quickly drew her hand away from him and in a quiet voice said, "I'm not sure you fully understand me, Oliver. I am not another Angelica."

"What do you mean by that?"

"I'm not liable to be an easy conquest. I have seen you and Angelica together. I know how she feels about her husband but I can promise you I have respect and love for mine."

"I'm not surprised to hear you say that," the young doctor told her. "But I am surprised that you have misunderstood me so. I have the most honorable of intentions."

"I want to believe that," she said.

"You must!" he insisted. "And you must not get wrong ideas about my friendship with Angelica. The overtures have been wholly on her part and I have kept up a pretense through not wanting to embarrass her. I promise you there is no love affair involved, though there could be if I wanted to have it so."

She listened to his serious declarations and pondered on whether the young doctor was telling the truth or not. He could be. It was hard to say. She told him, "I appreciate your concern for me but I do not think it is warranted. And I'm sure you must be wrong about my husband not returning to the hospital. It may be that he changed his mind."

"I doubt it," Dr. Rush said bitterly. "And I am truly worried about you. As you have probably discovered for yourself, this is a very strange house with strange things happening in it."

"I cannot deny that."

"There is something very wrong here," he went on. "I'm not certain what. But I know that this is true."

She gave a tiny shudder as she stared at the dark bulk of the great mansion rising above them in the advancing night. She said, "From the first moment I arrived here the house has had a depressing effect on me."

"Not much wonder."

"If you feel that way why do you remain here?" she asked.

"Because I happen to be working under your husband," he said. "It is the usual arrangement that his junior assistant live here under the same roof with him."

"He is a fine surgeon, isn't he?"

"The best," the young man said. "I have learned a great deal from him. But there are those at the hospital who whisper about him and say that he has changed."

"Changed?"

"Since his illness," the young man said too carefully.

She gazed at him in the darkness. The shadows around them gave her the courage to say, "Don't you mean his cocaine addiction?"

"Then you know?" he sounded surprised.

"Yes. I know."

"And it doesn't make any difference?"

"Not to me now," she said. "It happened before I came here. I'm sure he's cured."

"There are some at the hospital not so sure."

"Dr. Farrow seems to have no doubts."

He said, "There is a reason for that. Dr. Farrow is his good friend."

"I'm still certain that Terence has overcome his addiction."

"It is possible," the young doctor said. "But in that case how do you explain his setting out at night in this way, assuming he didn't go to the hospital?"

"But you are the one who assumed that," she told him.

"You are quite right," he said. "It seems that I cannot shake your faith in your husband."

"Was that your wish?"

"No," he said. "Not really. I only wish to help you in any way I can. I think you are one of the finest people I've ever met."

"Thank you, Oliver," she said. "I appreciate your high opinion of me though I have serious doubts that I warrant it."

"Please remember," he told her, "I am always at your command."

"I'll remember," she promised. "And it may be that I shall one day need such a friend."

He saw her to the door and then walked off into the darkness alone. She watched him go and decided that he was probably a young man of much more character than she realized. And it was good to know that she had one such staunch friend in the old mansion. But as she entered the reception hall she was greeted by a grim-faced Angelica and knew that the blond young woman must have discovered that she was in the garden with Dr. Rush.

Angelica's cold blue eyes fastened on her. She said, "You were out there a long while."

"Yes."

"Weren't you afraid of being in the dark alone? With all the dreadful things that are happening?"

Susan said, "As it turned out I wasn't alone."

"Indeed?" Angelica's voice was filled with sarcasm.

"No. Dr. Rush came to join me for a little."

"How pleasant for you," Angelica said with pointed sarcasm.

"Yes, it was," she said, having decided to remain very calm about it.

"Where is he now?" Angelica wanted to know.

"I have no idea," she said. "He walked away by himself."

"I see," the blond young woman said.

Susan lost no time making her way upstairs. She didn't much appreciate having been given this third degree by her sister-in-law. And she could tell that Angelica was livid about the young doctor paying her even that small attention. It was a strange situation. She reached their suite and saw that Sally had turned down her bed and set out lamps in both the parlor and the bedroom.

Now began her long vigil. Terence had promised to return as early as possible but the minutes went by and then the hours and he still did not return. By ten o'clock she was in a state of great agitation. It began to seem all too likely that he had gone off on some wild orgy rather than visiting the hospital as he'd said.

She paced up and down in the softly lighted parlor conscious of the ticking of the great grandfather clock in one corner of the room. Several times she went to the window to see if there might be any sign of his carriage returning. But there was only the darkness. She became extremely disconsolate and nervous.

The night grew older and she was reaching a high peak of nervous tension. All at once she heard the sound of someone in the corridor outside. Thinking that it might be her husband she threw open the door and looked eagerly out into the dimly lighted corridor for a sign of him. But despite the sound she'd heard the corridor was now seemingly empty.

She called out, "Terry?"

There was no reply. Just eerie silence. But she was positive she had heard someone out there. Now she timidly advanced into the corridor itself and moved along it a little distance. It was then she heard a kind of shuffling sound, but this time from behind her. She happened to glance up at the wall and saw the dark shadow of a figure looming behind her with a hand raised holding what appeared to be a scalpel!

"No!" she screamed and turned around.

Standing there was a drunken Phillip Ward. As soon as she screamed he lowered his hand, which as she'd suspected, contained a surgeon's scalpel.

"Don't have to be afraid," he assured her drunkenly as he stood there in his dressing-gown swaying slightly.

"What are you doing out here with that knife?" she demanded.

"Knife?" he gazed at the weapon in his hand stupidly. "That is a fine surgical instrument!"

"I don't care what it is," she said. "You shouldn't be roaming about the house flourishing it!"

"Sorry," the stout man said with a guilty look on the florid face with the large gray mustache. "I sort of got carried away I guess."

"You almost frightened me to death," she said.

"No need to fear me," he said in the same slurred fashion but she thought there was a strange, mad gleam in his eyes.

She told him, "You should go straight back to your room and put that away." She indicated the scalpel.

He nodded. "You won't tell Angelica or any of the others, will you?" His tone was pleading.

"Not if you go at once."

"I'll go," he promised. And he did.

Only when she'd returned to her own suite did she realize the strain those few minutes had been for her. The drunken Phillip had given her a nasty fright and in spite of her brazening it out she now felt the results of it. Glancing at the clock she saw that is was almost midnight and decided to give up waiting for Terry to return.

She felt she should go to bed even if she weren't able to sleep. She would at least get some rest from this pacing up and down. The chances seemed strong that her husband would not return until the morning or perhaps later. It was a tormenting business and she was helpless to do anything but wait.

After slowly preparing for bed she put out the lamps in the parlor and in their bedroom. She lay in bed staring up into the darkness and still waiting for some sound of the missing Terry. But no sounds came and after a while she dropped off into an uneasy sleep.

She began to dream and in her dream she was running across the lawn of Willowgate pursued by a dark figure with a scalpel in his hand. She was screaming for help and sobbing but no one seemed to hear her. She reached the passage through the bushes leading to the estate of Dr. Farrow and made her escape through it. Then she ran on to the formidable Tudor mansion and pounded on the door to be admitted.

"Let me in!" she pleaded. "Please let me in!"

She turned at the same time to stare back into the night and see if her pursuer was drawing close to her. But the figure seemed to have vanished. The Jack the Ripper of her nightmare had faded into the darkness.

Suddenly the door opened and at the sight of the figure standing there her mouth gaped open and she stumbled back with a terrified sob. It was Dr. Donald Farrow with a scalpel in his hand and a maniacal smile on his usually stern face. He came slowly toward her!

Chapter Six

Susan wakened from her nightmare screaming. Then she sat up in bed trembling as an aftermath of her terrifying dream. She was perspiring and the nightmare was as vivid in her mind as if it had actually happened. As a child she'd been prone to this sort of bad dream but she'd grown out of them. Apparently the ordeal of being in the old mansion had brought them back once again.

She sat up in bed, not aware of the hour but acutely aware that it was long after midnight at least, and also that her husband had not yet returned. The place in the bed beside her was empty. After a little she got out of bed and put on her slippers and dressing gown. She lit a candle in a candle holder which Sally had left on her bedside table for any emergencies.

Now with the candle in hand she advanced into the parlor. She wanted to be sure that Terence wasn't there. Often he would roam about in the dark. But he wasn't anywhere in the suite. She went to the door leading to the hallway and opened it cautiously. She saw that the night lamp which usually offered a small amount of light for the area had been extinguished.

Stepping out into the corridor she suddenly felt a cool breeze flow around her. At the same instant she knew a weird kind of fear. It was almost as if a ghostly hand had touched her. It was uncanny and she couldn't stifle the feeling. Her concern subsided as her actual fear increased. She had started back to her suite when something interrupted her.

It came from above. Someone calling to her, "Susan!"

She halted with her lovely oval face showing alarm in the flickering glow of the candle. She called out, "Who is it?"

Once again from the stairway area and above came the soft, neutral voice, calling, "Susan!"

Now she slowly made her way to the landing, still keeping the candle in her hand. The voice had come from somewhere on the next landing. She stood there gazing up the second long flight of stairs but was unable to see anything at the top of them but the darkness.

Again she called out, "Who is there?"

"Come and find out," the neutral voice said.

She hesitated and then slowly began to ascend the stairs. Her mind was divided about what she was doing. One part of it was crying out a frantic warning to her, the other urged her to go on and see who it might be waiting for her up there in the shadows.

Reaching the top of the stairs, she halted, and asked, "Where are you?"

She'd not finished asking this when the phantom figure swooped out of the shadows at her. She'd seen its head and shoulders before and recognized it at once. The shrouded face, a face already in the first stages of decay, the damp-grave smell of the gray, flowing shroud. These were all the impressions she had time to form. In that instant the phantom strongly shoved her back so that she toppled down the stairs to crash in a crumpled heap at the first landing. She felt a dreadful pain in her left arm and at once passed out.

When she came to the pain was still there in her arm and a troubled-looking Terence was bending over her. He said, "How did this happen?"

"You're back!" she said, staring at him in a stunned fashion.

"Yes, I'm back," he exclaimed impatiently. "But what about you?"

The pain in her left arm was a throbbing torment, making it almost impossible for her to think. Gritting her teeth, she said, "I saw the ghost!"

"What ghost?"

"Ruth's!"

"Stop it!" he commanded angrily. "I can't accept that nonsense from you!"

She closed her eyes and groaned. "My arm!"

"What about it?" He reached for her left arm.

"Easy!" she cried as she winced under the pain of his touching it.

"Seems like a simple fracture of the lower arm," he said. "You're lucky! You could have broken your neck instead of your arm. Those stairs are steep!"

He then lifted her up and carried her back into their suite. Placing her gently on her bed he went about lighting the lamp and getting water and cloths and material for splints and bandages. In the interim she lay there gasping with pain.

Terence came back and set her arm and bound it in place. Only then did its worst throbbing ease a little. He said, "Now, please explain how you came to fall down that flight of stairs."

She looked at him tearfully. "I've already told you. I saw the ghost."

"What has that to do with your fall?"

"I didn't fall. The ghost pushed me down the stairs or I fell back in fear! It amounts to the same thing."

"I disagree," her doctor husband said evenly. "I think you went up there for some reason and became terrified and missed your step and toppled down."

"No!" she protested.

Terence sat on her bed looking weary and forlorn. "Go on," he said. "Give me your version of it then."

"I heard my name called from up there."

"Did you recognize the voice?"

"No."

"Was it a man's or a woman's? Surely you can tell that."

"I can't," she said. "It was a strange voice. Like a ghostly voice and I suppose that is what it was."

"Go on," he said impatiently.

"I decided to go up and see who it was."

"And?"

"I reached the top of the stairs and I couldn't see anyone."

"What then?"

"I was about to go across the landing in search of the owner of the voice when all at once the phantom materialized."

"What sort of phantom?"

"A woman with a shroud. The veils of the shroud hid her face but not enough to conceal the decay that had set in. I could smell the grave about her. I was too horrified to defend myself as she shoved me backward!"

Terence scowled at her. "You surely don't expect me to give credence to a story like that?"

"It's what happened."

"You must have been sleepwalking. It was probably a part of a nightmare!"

"No," she protested. "I did have a nightmare but it was just before all this happened."

"And I say the nightmare went on to end only when you fell down the stairs."

"You'll never make me agree to that," she told him, the pain in her arm still tormenting her.

"I could accept that sort of story from some little maid or

other ignorant creature but not from my wife!"

She said, "I was attacked by a phantom. Ruth's phantom!"

Terry looked at her almost angrily. "And why do you persist in saying it was Ruth's ghost?"

Her eyes met his. "Because I have seen her before."

"Before?"

"Yes."

"Where?"

"In this room for one place," she said. "She came and showed herself in the doorway. I didn't tell you because I didn't want to distress you."

"A likely story!"

"It's so," she persisted. "And then she came again when I was away from the room. And that time she left a sign."

Her husband's eyebrows raised. "A sign?"

"Yes."

"What sort of sign?"

She looked at him earnestly, then said, "She left a bouquet of artificial violets. A bouquet which your sister Samantha made for her. It was placed in her dead hands and buried with her and I found it on my dresser."

"Do you expect me to believe that?"

"I do," she said. "And I can prove it."

"I very much doubt that," her husband said grimly. "I find this talk of Ruth deplorable. It is not good taste to speak of the dead in this way."

"I still have those violets," she told him. "In one of the dresser drawers."

He shook his head. "I don't want to see them."

She was triumphant now despite her pain. She said, "Let me show you." And she slowly moved to the edge of the bed and got to her feet. Then she crossed to the dresser and opened the drawer and stood by it.

"Well?" her husband said; he had come to stand by her.

She looked up at him with blank dismay. "They're gone! The violets are gone!"

"They were never there," he said.

"They were!" she protested. "Someone has taken them!"

"Who would know where they were?"

"I can't say," she admitted in a despairing tone as she gazed into the empty lower drawer again.

"I admire your trying to convince me," he said. "But surely you see that it's hopeless."

"No!" she cried, turning to him as she suddenly remembered.

"What now?" he asked with some annoyance.

"I still can prove I found the violets."

"How?"

"I have a witness."

"A witness?"

"Yes. Your sister Samantha saw the violets and identified them. It was she who made up the bouquet for the coffin."

"Samantha saw these violets?" he said, sounding wary.

"Yes, You can ask her!"

"Not tonight," he said. "Fortunately the rest of the house hasn't been wakened despite all the noise. It can wait until the morning."

Painfully she made her way back to the bed. "You will see that I am right," she said.

"Let us not worry about it now," he told her as he helped cover her with the bed clothing. "Is your arm bad?"

"It seems to be easing."

"I'm sure that it will," he said. "You'll have to wear the bandages and splints until it heals. But that will be more a nuisance than actually painful. However, you can expect some pain for the first few days."

She stared up at him. "Where were you until this hour?"

"I thought you'd get around to that," he said grimly.

"Well?"

"I was at the hospital," he said.

"I can't believe it!"

"Then ask Farrow," he said. "Shortly after I went to the hospital this evening a poor devil was brought in who'd been run over by one of the Dover stagecoaches. He'd been drinking and lurched in front of the horses before the driver could bring them to a halt."

"Go on," she said, still not sure.

"We began working on him. He had more bruises and broken bones than you can imagine. But the worst injury was a head injury. One of the horse's shoes had caught him on the back of the head and crushed the bone like an eggshell. It was damage that couldn't wait to be repaired. The pressure had to be removed. The only answer was to take him to the operating table. Farrow and I worked on him until after one o'clock. But we saved his life. With some luck he'll live and be not too much the worse for it all. A few years ago he would have surely died."

The details of his story were too real to have been made up, she decided. And he mentioned having Dr. Farrow to confirm all that he'd told her. She knew she would have to accept his explanation and forgive him.

She said, "I'm beginning to learn what it means to be a doctor's wife."

"It is not an easy role to play," he told her. "But I'm certain you will measure up to it."

"I wonder," she said.

"Now you must try and sleep," he told her as he began to undress for bed.

The following morning was bright and sunny. She awoke

early and almost forgot her broken left arm until she moved. Then she winced. Terence was already up and dressed. Now he came to her and checked her arm and helped her sit up in bed.

With a smile, he said, "Breakfast in bed for you today, young lady."

"I could go downstairs!" she said.

"It would be a strain and there's no need. The less moving about you do for a few days the better."

He summoned Sally and gave the maid her breakfast order. Then when Sally went to get it he sat down with Susan once again. He said, "I want you to stop all this useless worrying and rid your mind of that ghost business."

"I can't help what I've seen," she said.

"All a product of your vivid imagination," he said, with a professional bedside suavity.

"I'll not be put off that easily," Susan told him. "I want you to bring Samantha here so I can prove to you that I found that bouquet of artificial violets."

He took on a resigned look. "Must I?"

"Please," she said. "Bring Samantha here."

"Wait until you've had breakfast."

"And you'll be gone by then," she reproached him. "No, bring her here now."

"Very well," he said. He pulled the bell cord again and after a few minutes the maid, Sally, returned. "Would you please find Miss Samantha and bring her here," he ordered her.

"Yes, sir," the girl said and went to find Samantha.

Terence got up and began to pace uneasily in the area by her bed. He said, "I don't like this at all!"

"It will be all right," she promised.

"We shouldn't need Samantha to settle our problems."

"This is a special case."

He frowned. "When we first met I distinctly recall your saying that you did not believe in ghosts."

"That was before I saw Willowgate and experienced certain things here," she said.

He halted and stared at her. "I should have told you about Ruth and what happened to her when we first met. It was a bad error on my part to try and conceal it."

"You tried to hide too many things," she replied quietly.

His face paled and he resumed pacing. She noted that in spite of her pointed comment he had not made any attempt to speak frankly about his cocaine addiction. It seemed that he did not even want to think about that.

There was the sound of footsteps and then Samantha, clad in black as usual, entered the room. She stood there an austere, gaunt figure. Gazing at Susan's bandaged arm, she asked, "What has happened to you?"

With a frown Terence quickly said, "She had a nasty fall. She broke her arm."

"Fall?" Samantha registered surprise. "Where?"

"On the stairs," he said, speaking up quickly again. "So she'll be mostly confined to her room for a few days."

"I'm so sorry," Samantha consoled her. "Those steps are treacherous. I have almost fallen more than once and I'm forever terrified that Father will topple down them, though he hasn't so far."

"The good luck of the mad," Terence said grimly.

Samantha gave him an indignant glance. "I don't think you should speak about our father in that derisive tone," she said.

"Sorry," he apologized. "We've called you in here to help us settle a small matter."

"Oh?" The gaunt woman seemed astonished.

Now Susan spoke up, "It's very simple, Samantha. It concerns the other day. You will remember that I was standing here holding a bouquet of violets and you came in and identified them."

Samantha's eyebrows raised. "Violets?"

"Yes, artificial violets which you made for Ruth," she said.

The gaunt woman nodded. "Yes. I did make a bouquet for the coffin. She was so fond of violets."

Encouraged, she said, "So surely you recall my finding them on the dresser and asking you about them."

Samantha looked uneasy. "When was that?"

"Just a day or so ago," Terence said impatiently. "Do you or do you not remember?"

"I'm sorry," Samantha said uneasily. "I don't recall seeing any bouquet in your hands, Susan. I placed those flowers in the coffin."

Susan stared at the gaunt woman in astonishment. "You can't mean that!"

"I'm sorry," Samantha said. And turning to Terence she said, "Please excuse me. I have to see Baker about something." And she left the room.

Susan turned to her husband in consternation. "It simply doesn't make any sense. She was here in this room! She saw the bouquet."

Her handsome, doctor husband stood there with a strange expression on his face. "That is not what she told us just now."

"I don't care what she said," she protested. "I know she was lying for some reason."

He frowned. "I don't like to think that."

"Then you doubt everything I've told you about seeing the ghost?"

Terence hesitated. "I think we should drop the subject for

a little. It is much too contentious."

Susan felt helpless and frustrated. She said, "It makes me feel you doubt me in everything."

"That is not true!"

"I'll somehow prove to you that Samantha was lying," she said. "I don't know just how at the moment but I'll find a way."

He said, "I'm going to be late at the hospital if I remain here talking any longer. Remember, don't move about too much today. Otherwise you're going to find that arm very painful."

Terence bent and kissed her good-bye but she felt that a kind of barrier had been raised between them. His doubt of her and her inability to make her story about the ghost seem true had produced a strain in their relationship.

After Terence left she lay in bed worrying about it all and wondering why Samantha had behaved as she had. She was deep in these thoughts when the blond Angelica came into the bedroom. Her sister-in-law stood at the foot of the bed and gave her a coldly appraising glance.

"So you had an accident last night," Angelica said.

"Yes."

"What happened?"

She gave the blond girl a grim look. "If I told you I'm certain you'd question my truthfulness just the same as the others."

"Not necessarily," Angelica said.

"I saw the ghost," Susan told her. "She shoved me down the stairs. Are you ready to accept that?"

Angelica shrugged. "I have heard stranger stories about this house."

"Thank you for that small bit of support," she said in a wry voice.

"What does Terence think about your arm?"

Susan studied her splinted arm. "He thinks it just a simple break. But it's painful enough."

"How did he react to your ghost story?" There was a mocking note in the blond girl's voice.

Susan looked down at the bedspread. "He didn't believe any of it."

"I'm not surprised."

"Why?"

Angelica said, "Because it concerns Ruth. He does not like to think of her as dead. I'm sure he's very sensitive on that point."

"He didn't seem to want to discuss it at all."

"I know," Angelica said with a suggestion of hidden meaning in her manner. "I believe he is more than a little mad on the subject of Ruth's murder."

"Really?"

"He's never been quite himself since he had that breakdown," Angelica went on. "The police were very suspicious of him, you know."

"Why?"

Angelica raised her eyebrows. "Because Ruth was a victim of Jack the Ripper and the Ripper is known to be a man with medical training."

She gasped. "You're not suggesting that Terence might have killed Ruth and committed those other murders as well?"

"Of course not," the blond girl told her. "I'm just pointing out that anyone in the area with medical knowledge could be thought of as suspect."

Susan said, "Then why not consider Terence's father? He is old and mad and possesses great skill as a surgeon. He also manages to elude Baker every so often!"

"I suppose he might be guilty," Angelica considered.

"Or Phillip?" Susan said. "Your husband gave me a scare last night when he approached me in a drunken state with a scalpel in his hand. Why wouldn't the police be suspicious of him?"

Angelica smiled coldly. "Probably because they believed he didn't have the brains or nerve to carry out such a task." And then she added, "But they could be wrong."

"Have you seen Ruth's ghost?" she asked.

"Almost everyone here has," her sister-in-law said. "Only Terence insists on denying it. And this makes you wonder about his mental condition."

The blond girl remained to talk for a few minutes longer and then left. Susan had been puzzled by the girl's talk and general behavior. She was left with the feeling that Angelica hated even the memory of Ruth and blamed her for much of Terence's problems. Yet she had also seemed to suggest that Terence might be the infamous murderer known as Jack the Ripper. This shocked Susan since she'd had worries about the same thing.

Just now she was concerned about Samantha and why the gaunt woman had refused to back her up in her story about the finding of the ghostly bouquet. She also wondered where the bouquet had gone. Surely someone had entered the apartment and searched the dresser until he found it.

One of her chief concerns was the drug addiction which her husband was apparently still battling. She worried that he might be continuing to take cocaine and that this was the answer to his odd behavior and his several mysterious disappearances. She knew that Terence had been on drugs before his first wife's murder and this did put him in a bad light.

She heard a footstep and looked up to see that a frightened-looking Samantha had entered the room. The gaunt woman came to the foot of her bed and stood there with her hands clasped.

"I'm sorry," the older woman said.

Susan eyed her with reproach. "You ought to be!"

"I didn't mean to make it difficult for you," Samantha told her.

"You lied!"

Samantha nodded miserably. In a taut voice, she said, "I know."

"Why?"

"Because of Terence."

"What do you mean by that?" she demanded.

"I didn't want to upset him. He's been through enough."

Susan stared at her with bewilderment. "Don't you think he ought to know the truth? If Ruth's ghost is being seen here don't you think he ought to admit it?"

The gaunt woman shook her head. "I would not force it on him. I was afraid."

"So you made me look a liar."

"I didn't think you'd mind," Terence's sister faltered. "You knew I was doing it for him. If you love him you must be prepared to make some sacrifices for him."

"I'm not prepared to deny the truth," Susan said. "It was important to me that I prove I had seen Ruth's ghost and come upon the bouquet of violets. You made me out a liar or someone given to lunatic imaginings."

"Terence will forget all about it," Samantha insisted. "I don't want him to have another of his breakdowns. You know he was in the hospital after the murder. His trouble could return again. I know him better than you. I can see that in him."

She listened with some impatience. "You believe he might have another bout of mental illness?"

"I'm not sure he's all that well now," Samantha said earnestly. "You must try to help him. Don't plague him with stories about Ruth's ghost coming back."

Susan said bitterly, "It's not likely he'd pay much attention to me after the performance you gave this morning."

Samantha's pinched face bore an ashamed expression. "I didn't intend you any harm."

"You made me appear a liar or worse," Susan told her with some bitterness. "And you should be the last to deny the ghost since you were one of the first to speak to me about its appearances here."

"I was only thinking of my brother's welfare," the gaunt woman insisted.

"But you surely will at least admit to me that you saw the bouquet of violets here?"

Samantha hesitated. Then in a low voice said, "I saw them."

"And now they have vanished. Where?"

"I don't know!" the older woman seemed on the verge of panic.

"Ruth's ghostly hand left them here," Susan suggested, "so perhaps they were removed in the same way."

"Yes," Samantha said tensely. "But don't tell Terence that!"

"It seems to me he should be told."

"No! He is much too unhappy as it is. You can be his salvation. Don't try to torture him!" With this fervent plea the gaunt woman in black turned and fled from the room.

She left Susan in a bleak mood of resignation. There would be no help from Samantha in her efforts to prove that Ruth's ghost had attacked her. Nor could she count on any of the others. She lay back on her pillow and closed her eyes. The nagging pain of her injured arm prevented her getting a truly good rest but she had several catnaps.

Just after lunch she had an unexpected visitor. It was the aristocratic senior surgeon Dr. Donald Farrow who came to pay her an unexpected visit. Shown into the room by Sally, the stern-faced man briskly made his way to her bedside and placed his hat and walking stick on the table as he sat by her.

"This is a most lamentable circumstance, Mrs. Ward," he said at once.

She smiled ruefully. "I didn't expect to be a patient when I next saw you."

"Terence told me about your fall," Dr. Farrow went on with a slight frown. "I decided to cut short my usual afternoon walk to pay you this visit."

"That is very kind of you. Is it true that you and Terry were at the hospital late performing an operation?"

He nodded. "That is quite true."

"So my husband didn't lie to me this time."

"No, he did not," the older surgeon assured her. "I'm also sure his absence on that first night in London can somehow be adequately explained. He probably has some good reason for not wanting to tell you the truth about it as yet."

"I can't think of a reason which would justify his lying to me," she said.

"Be patient!" he urged her. "In time you may come to know and understand his actions."

"I hope so."

"About this fall," Dr. Farrow said. "How did it come about?"

Her face shadowed. "That is also a matter of controversy."

"Controversy?" his tone was astonished.

"Yes." And she told him, ending with Samantha's denying ever having seen the violet bouquet.

Dr. Farrow's aristocratic face was a study in consternation. He eyed her sharply. "You actually believe that you were attacked by Ruth's ghost?"

"Yes."

"And you told this to Terence?"

"I did."

"And he denied it?"

"He brushed the whole idea aside," she said wearily. "There seems to be a conspiracy of silence in this house where the ghost is concerned. Several of those living here have spoken to me about seeing the phantom, but when I ask them to testify to this they are quick in their denials."

The older surgeon frowned. "Your husband is a sensitive man. He does not want to think about the horror of Ruth's murder nor of the possibility of her unhappy spirit wandering about in this house. And, in all fairness, I suppose one cannot blame him for that."

"Am I not to have any consideration?" she asked.

"It is most unfortunate for you," he agreed quickly. "You are caught in a most unpleasant position. You have my sympathy! I will do all I can to make Terence listen to you."

"He must know that by remaining here I am exposing myself to grave danger."

"Perhaps he is closing his mind to that," Dr. Farrow said worriedly. "I will attempt to discuss this seriously with him today. And in the meanwhile you should get all the rest you can and avoid any sort of needless risk."

She gave him a wry glance. "I have been trying to do exactly that and I have not had much success."

"I realize that," he agreed with a sigh.

Susan gave him a questioning look. "Dr. Farrow, what do you honestly think? Do you believe my husband has given up the use of cocaine?"

He looked troubled. "That is a difficult question. And you

mustn't regard this cocaine thing in the wrong light. Terence came to use the drug through legitimate medical experimentation. There has been nothing criminal in his history of addiction."

"Does that make so much difference if he is left a madman by its influence?"

"Don't say such a thing!" the older doctor protested.

"I have to ask myself that question," she told him. "Why am I to be denied mentioning it to you?"

"I'm sorry," the stern Dr. Farrow said. "I understand your feelings even though I seem to deny them. In my own opinion Terence is cured. I can only ask you to take my word for it."

"Thank you, Doctor," she said, grateful for this small easing of her fears.

He left her shortly afterward and she again closed her eyes and sought to escape in sleep. She managed better than she had in the morning and sank into a period of deep slumber which must have lasted more than an hour. When she finally wakened she pulled the bell cord for Sally and waited for the girl to come. But the maid with the yellow pigtails apparently wasn't at her station and so missed the call. Rather impatiently Susan tried the cord with her good hand once again.

It was close to five in the evening and she wanted to wash and dress for the return of her husband. With her arm in the splints she needed Sally's assistance. She was waiting for the girl and feeling slightly worried when she heard footsteps outside in the hallway.

All at once she was filled with an unreasoning fear. As the door to the bedroom edged open her fear mounted rather than subsided and she saw the bent figure of the mad, white-bearded Simon Ward suddenly show itself. There was an insane gleam in the old man's eyes as he came purposefully toward her bed!

Chapter Seven

Startled by the unexpected appearance of the mad old doctor Susan sat up in bed and told him, "You shouldn't be down here, Dr. Ward."

The bent old man with the long white hair and white beard halted at the foot of her bed and, in a mild voice which was in striking contrast to his appearance, said, "You have no need to be afraid of me, my dear."

In spite of her fear she suddenly felt ashamed. She realized that she was being just as intolerant as the others in the gloomy old house. She had accused her husband and the rest of being too strict in regard to keeping Dr. Simon Ward a prisoner in the attic.

She said, "Why have you come to my room?"

"I heard of your accident," he said, his eyes still showing a strange gleam; but nothing else was strange about his demeanor.

"Oh?"

"You broke your arm in a fall on the stairs, so I was told," he went on.

"That is true."

"The stairs are too steep," he said. "I have had several close calls on them."

"Really?" She was still very apprehensive.

He made no move to come closer. "Did my son set the break and splint it properly?"

"Yes."

"Let me see," he said. And now he came up beside her and

took her arm gently to inspect it. She saw that his fingernails had grown to the length of talons and the backs of his hands were covered with thick, iron-gray hair.

She said, "My arm is feeling much better."

"He has done an excellent job," the old man told her. "My son is a talented doctor."

"I fully agree," she replied.

His bearded face showed a sad smile. "Your name is Susan. Isn't that right?"

"Yes."

"Baker reminded me of that," he said. "I had been calling you Ruth. And Ruth is dead, of course."

"Yes. She is dead."

The old man took a few steps away from her bed as if he were going to leave the room. She hoped that he would because even though he was in a mild, lucid mood his presence there made her nervous. Yet she felt it only right that she should be tolerant of him. He had been a fine doctor in his day.

The gleaming eyes fixed on her and he hesitated. "Ruth's spirit still lingers in this house."

"I know you've said that."

"She met an unhappy death. Jack the Ripper murdered her, you know."

"So I've heard," she said.

"It was very tragic. We all were shocked. Especially my son Terence."

"I'm sure of that."

"It was right after the Ripper murdered Elizabeth Stride; the papers say that she was nicknamed Long Liz. But the Ripper was interrupted in his work by a man who drove a pony cart into the yard. The pony shied as it entered the yard, probably because Jack the Ripper was hidden in a dark corner behind the gate. When the driver of the cart jumped down and lifted the woman's head, the blood was still pouring from her throat."

The old man's words and the rapt expression on his ancient face sent a chill down her spine. In a taut voice, she said, "You seem very well acquainted with the details of the crime."

Those too-bright eyes remained fixed on her. He nodded. "Yes. I have made myself familiar with the actions of the Ripper on that night. The interruption must have annoyed him for within an hour he trailed Ruth into the courtyard where she was searching for the home of a nurse and attacked her."

"On that same night?"

"Yes," the old man said. "After he cut Ruth's throat he went on to carve up the rest of her body. Then he fled after wiping his bloody hands and knife on the skirt of her dress. It was a hellish piece of work!"

"Please!" she begged him. "I'd rather not hear any more of the details."

"I beg your pardon," he said. "I forgot you have not my medical training. Such things are commonplace to me. In my lifetime I have spent thousands of hours at the operating table. Carving human flesh is quite an ordinary practice when one is trained for it."

She said, "And the Ripper apparently had your training."

"Yes," the old man said. "I think he must be a surgeon."

She was about to query him some more when an agitated Baker showed himself in the doorway of the room. "Dr. Ward! You were warned not to come down here!" the old servant said.

The demented Simon Ward gave him a mocking glance. "I have done no harm."

"You've probably frightened this young lady out of her wits," Baker protested, coming up beside him and taking him by the arm to lead him away. Baker turned to her to add, "I'm sorry, Mrs. Ward, I try to watch him but he's a slippery one!"

"It's all right," she said. "We had a pleasant conversation, didn't we, Dr. Ward?"

The old man gave the servant a proud look. "You see! At least there is one person in this house who still appreciates me!"

"We all appreciate you, sir," Baker said. "But it is time you returned upstairs again."

Simon Ward's bearded face showed a sad expression as he glanced at her in farewell. "Mind what I told you about the Ripper, my dear. He is still on the lookout for new victims!"

"You mustn't mind him, Mrs. Ward," Baker said with mild anger. And he hurried the old man out of the room.

There were no more intrusions on her. At dinnertime Terence came to see her. He'd come home early from the hospital for once. He came directly to their apartment.

After he'd greeted her with a kiss he gave her a box of candy and asked her, "How did your day go?"

"Fairish," she said. "Your father managed to get down here and talk to me."

He at once became angry. "Where was Baker at the time? He's supposed to keep a close watch on my father."

"Somehow he eluded him."

"That shouldn't happen," Terence said with his Byronic features clouded.

"It's nothing to make a big case about," she said. "I really didn't mind."

Her husband's eyebrows lifted. "Did he behave all that well?"

"Yes. He was quite lucid and interesting in his talk."

"That's unusual," he said with a hint of disbelief in his tone.

"It's true," she said.

"I'm surprised."

"So was I. Pleasantly," she said. "Though he did mention Jack the Ripper and went on rather wildly about him."

Terence at once frowned. "What did he say?"

She was astounded by his nervous reaction. She said, "He told me about what had gone on before the Ripper encountered Ruth on the night he'd murdered her. The only thing wrong was that he was rather gory in the details and he apologized for that."

"I should think he would," her husband said, completely upset. "I hope you didn't allow him to bother you too much."

"No. Baker came to my rescue and took him away."

Her husband began to pace up and down restlessly at the foot of her bed. "Try to wipe your mind clean of whatever he said. It was probably all imagined on his part."

"I doubt that," she argued. "He seemed to have quite an excellent grasp of how the Ripper hunted out his victim, what he did to them."

Terence halted and stared at her. She saw that his face was pale. "My father is mad! You should know better than to listen to him!"

"Even madmen have their lucid moments. I'm positive he was having one during his visit down here."

"A likely story!" her husband said with impatience.

"I truly believe it," she insisted. "I don't know how to explain his knowledge of the Ripper and what that murderer has done, but he did appear to have a lot of facts."

"Facts contrived in his sick mind," Terence told her.

"He was complimentary of the way you treated my arm," she said.

Her handsome husband looked mildly pleased on hearing this. He said, "He did notice?"

"Of course," she said. "He was on his best behavior."

"I still don't like the idea of his escaping and roaming about at will. He could do harm to himself, not considering others."

"I'm sure Baker does his best," she said, defending the old manservant. "Your father can be wily when he likes."

"I know," Terence said.

Nothing more of consequence happened that evening. In fact it was the beginning of a period of peacefulness in the old house. Susan began to have guilty feelings about her fears and to doubt all the evidence which had pointed to her being attacked by a ghost. She found herself wondering if perhaps her husband and the others had not been right. Maybe she had imagined a shadow into a ghostly figure. Perhaps she had been the victim of her too-vivid imagination.

Several days and nights passed without event. The dressing on her arm had been changed so that now only small splints supported the broken bone. Most of the pain had vanished and she was able to walk about freely. Only the injured arm and hand were limited in use. Terence had another busy spell at the hospital and was often absent from the old mansion at night as well as during the day.

She had to depend on the other members of the family for company and on the young intern, Dr. Oliver Rush. One evening when he arrived at Willowgate he approached her and said, "I have tickets for the Albion Theater this evening. I know that your husband is going to be at the hospital until late and I wondered if you might be willing to accompany me to the play?"

Susan found herself embarrassed. She said, "Surely there is someone else you can ask."

"Who?" the young doctor inquired wryly. "Angelica's husband is at home every night. Your sister-in-law Samantha never attends the theater. I even spoke to your husband about the possibility of your accompanying me."

She was surprised. "What did he say?"

Dr. Rush smiled. "He was quite willing that you should attend if it was your wish. He had no objections."

"I see," she said, not knowing how to cope with this unexpected approval on the part of Terence. "You are sure he won't be home until late?"

"I'm positive of it," the young doctor said. "He operated on a patient this morning. One of those brain operations and now he and Dr. Farrow are watching the patient. They've been at his bedside all afternoon and your husband plans to be there observing until midnight when Dr. Farrow will take over alone."

"Is the patient apt to die?"

"I think not," Dr. Rush said. "But it is an interesting case so they are making notes on the changes in his condition for a record to read later to the college of surgeons."

She offered the young man a sad smile. "My husband is a most dedicated man."

"And you, if I may say so, are a most neglected wife," Dr. Rush said. "Let me help make amends. You have hardly left this house since you arrived."

"That is so," she agreed.

"We can have an early dinner and take the coach for the theater and arrive in time," the young man went on. "Please say that you will attend the performance with me."

A roguish twinkle showed in her eyes. "Well, why not?" she said. "But I shall have to hurry to dress and be ready to leave on time."

"But you always look enchanting," was the young

man's friendly protest.

Susan found herself excited at the prospect of getting away from the gloomy old mansion for a little. She would have preferred the excursion to have been in the company of her husband. But to go with Dr. Oliver Rush would be enjoyable. And she need have no qualms since the young doctor had already spoken to Terence and received his permission to take her to the theater.

She selected an especially attractive blue gown and made her way down to dinner early. She found Angelica and her husband, Phillip, already there waiting for her arrival. Angelica had all too clearly heard the news and now greeted her coldly.

The blond young woman said, "Do you think it proper to attend the theater with Dr. Rush?"

Knowing of the blonde's jealousy for the young man, Susan said, "Terence has given his permission."

This surprised Angelica but she quickly covered up her feelings and coldly said, "You may know that but what will strangers think? Your appearing with a strange man at the theater is bound to give rise to gossip."

Susan said, "Oliver is my husband's associate and not a stranger. I very much doubt if our attending the play together will cause any talk."

Phillip beamed at her over his whiskey glass. "I agree with you. Time you had a change. This house can be a grim place after a while."

His wife gave the stout man a withering look. "I wish you could be as thoughtful of me!"

"I have enough of London during the day," Phillip Ward told his blond wife. "When I get home I am content to rest and enjoy your company."

"What of me?" Angelica demanded. "Don't you think I

ever tire of Willowgate?"

The stout brother of Terence shrugged. "You are free to visit the city whenever you like. We are, in fact, living in a section of the city. I make no rules for you; I simply ask that I have my evenings to myself."

"You prefer to drink during your non-working hours," his wife said angrily.

This argument might have continued had not Dr. Rush presented himself. As he joined them it was clear that he had dressed especially for the outing. His white tie and tails marked it as a special occasion for him. Phillip offered him a drink which the young man accepted.

Angelica took her aside and said, "Are you certain that Terence has given his approval of this outing?"

"Dr. Rush told me he has and I see no reason to doubt his word," Susan replied.

"I don't like any of it," the blond woman said. "I trust you won't come to regret your decision."

Susan was not upset about the dire predictions of her new sister-in-law since she realized that it was jealousy of the young doctor that prompted her words. All during their early dinner Angela continued to make cutting remarks which both Susan and the doctor chose to ignore. Samantha remained grimly silent. At last they finished the meal and were free to leave. Phillip remained seated at the head of the table, glassy-eyed from drink.

When they reached the front door she saw that it was drizzling. At once she rang for Sally and had the maid find her crimson cape and cloak and bring it down to her. As Dr. Oliver Rush helped her don the cape she saw Sally's eyes fixed on it as she stood by. It was then that Susan recalled how much the maid had liked the cloak. And that she'd even been caught trying it on one day.

There was a carriage waiting for them. The young doctor had gone to the stables and ordered it as soon as she'd agreed to accompany him to the play. Now they sat together in the shadowed interior of the vehicle as it drove out of the grounds of Willowgate to clatter over the cobblestoned streets on their way to the theater.

She glanced at her companion in the near darkness of the interior of the carriage and asked, "What is the name of the play we are seeing tonight?"

"It's a melodrama," Dr. Rush told her. "I believe it bears the title of *The Tragedy of Lady Audrey*. It is one of the hits in the West End."

"I haven't heard about it," she said. "But I'm sure it will prove interesting."

"It is bound to with you as my companion," he said gallantly.

"I forget that we are here in London," she said. "So much has happened since my arrival. There has been such confusion!"

"I understand," he said.

They neared the center of the old city and were slowed down by the traffic. Gas lamps burned brightly on the street corners and well-dressed gentlemen and their ladies strolled along the sidewalks with umbrellas held over them. Occasionally one caught a glimpse of a red-jacketed member of Her Majesty's forces in golden helmet decorated with white plumes.

Street hawkers of all kinds were busy vending their wares as they moved freely among the crowded groups on the sidewalks before the theaters. The carriage came to a halt and Dr. Rush helped her out. They managed to cross the sidewalk and enter the busy lobby.

"What an exciting place to be!" she gasped.

The tall young doctor looked down at her, pleased. "You had better thank the rich patient who saw that I was given the tickets as a gift!"

They joined the throng entering the stalls and she saw that though it was raining the ladies were dressed in bright patterns and gaily decorated bonnets to match, while many of their escorts wore evening clothes as Dr. Rush did. They found their seats, which were almost in the center of the theater and about a third of the way back from the stage.

Susan was pleasantly excited at the prospect of the play with all her doubts and uncertain fears thrust in the background of her mind.

Then the curtain rose and the play began. It did not take Susan long to become aware of the source of the play's plot. It dealt with a wealthy lady of title whose husband was leading a double life. As it was revealed that he prowled the dark streets of London's underworld as a depraved killer on certain nights and lived as a respectable member of the aristocracy the balance of the time, she realized the play had been based on the strange career of Jack the Ripper.

When, the curtain dropped on the first act she turned to Dr. Rush and in a taut voice asked him, "Did you know the subject of the play when you invited me to see it?"

The young man looked uncomfortable. "Upon my word, I didn't," he protested.

"You're certain of that?" she said, studying him with a good deal of suspicion.

"All I knew was that it was a popular play," the young man said. He waved around at the crowded theater. "And you can see that this information was correct. There isn't an empty seat."

"The play is about Jack the Ripper, that's why!"

Dr. Rush crimsoned. "It may be. But I didn't know it at

the time I invited you to attend."

Susan was far from convinced that this was true. But she said no more about it. After the intermission the curtain went up on the thrilling melodrama once again and she gave her attention to the stage and the bravura performance of the cast. The second act ended with the titled murderer finally revealed to his wife as a criminal.

Dr. Rush stood up and asked her, "Would you like some tea and cakes? They're serving them in this area of the theater now."

"I will take tea," she said.

The young man signaled to a waitress and a few minutes later they were served. As they sat drinking the tea and enjoying the cakes, he asked her, "What do you think of the play?"

"It is well acted," she replied. "And perhaps the playwright's theory that the murderer is a man of title may be true."

"I agree," Dr. Rush said. "I think that is why the play is drawing such crowds. All London is interested in learning the identity of the Ripper."

"I had hoped never to hear the name again, to forget that such a monster existed."

"As long as the murders continue you'll hear about him," was the young doctor's prediction.

They finished their tea and the third-act curtain rose. Now the play gathered in intensity. Lady Audrey tried to protect her husband by hiding his guilt from the others in the family. But she was ill repaid for her attempts to save him. He turned on her in one of his mad fits and slit her throat. Fortunately, Lady Audrey's brother saw him do the foul deed and at once denounced him. The play ended with the suicide of the mad Lord Burchill.

As the playgoers slowly filed out of the theater Susan heard much discussion of the drama they'd just witnessed. Nearly everyone was convinced that they had seen a play based on the case of Jack the Ripper and many of them seemed to believe the playwright had some special secret information about the monster prowling London's streets at night.

One troubled dowager said, "But the Ripper has to be someone with medical training."

Her companion reminded her, "In the play Lord Burchill was a failed medical student."

"I had forgotten," the dowager admitted as she moved on by Susan and Dr. Rush.

Susan and the young doctor waited at the curb outside the theater for a few minutes as the carriages came along in single file. Their carriage was among the last to draw up by the theater entrance.

After they'd entered it and were comfortably seated in its dark interior, she said, "I expect that play will go on drawing crowds for months."

"Undoubtedly," Dr. Rush agreed.

There was a short period of silence between them broken only by the clatter of the horses' hooves on the cobblestone street and the creaking of the carriage wheels. She gave the young doctor another searching glance in the shadowed interior of the vehicle. She could barely see his face to note the serious expression showing on it.

She broke the silence by saying, "You know that several of the Ripper murders were committed in the area near Willowgate."

"Yes," he said, rather tensely.

"And that my husband's first wife, Ruth, was among the victims," she went on.

"I have heard that too."

"Did you also hear that Dr. John Morley, your predecessor as my husband's associate, was questioned concerning the murders and that he later killed himself?"

"Yes. I know about him as well."

"A great many people believed that he was Jack the Ripper," she told the young doctor in the carriage beside her.

"But he was not the only one in the house with medical knowledge," Dr. Rush said.

"True," she said. "There was my husband, his father, and you might even include his brother, Phillip."

"By all means," Dr. Rush said. "Phillip Ward was a medical student and he is familiar with surgical instruments since he sells them."

"I believe the police questioned my husband and everyone in the house."

"But they found nothing to suggest any of them might be Jack the Ripper?" the young doctor said.

"Apparently not," she said.

"And now the murders have resumed once again."

"Yes."

"The latest in the series took place the night you and Dr. Ward arrived in London," he said.

She sensed the pointedness in his statement and gave him a frightened glance. "You can't be suggesting that my husband is the Ripper?"

"Not at all," he replied at once, but without too much conviction in his tone. "It was just that the coincidence struck me."

She was again thinking of Terence's still unexplained absence of that particular night and of her own grim suspicions. There had been no Ripper murders while he had been in America. And there was his record of instability to consider, his addiction to cocaine which might or might not be cured.

She said, bitterly, "I'm afraid I must take the same stand Lady Audrey did in the play. I must protest my husband's innocence no matter how the facts point toward him."

"Lady Audrey died as a result of her efforts to save her husband," the young doctor said evenly.

Susan was convinced now that Dr. Oliver Rush had suspicions that Terence might be the Ripper. That was why he'd deliberately taken her to see this play, no doubt in an attempt to enlist her aid in clearing up the crimes. But she wasn't going to be twisted about as easily as that. She was not to be tricked into admitting that she'd entertained similar suspicions on her own.

Susan said, "Because I feel sure my husband is not a murderer I'm willing to take the risk of defending him."

The young man studied her anxiously in the semidarkness of the jolting carriage. "Then I can only pray that your confidence in Dr. Ward is justified."

Her eyes met his. "Then you believe him guilty?"

"I don't know what to believe."

"That is why you took me to that play tonight, isn't it?"

"Perhaps."

"I know it is," she said.

"If your husband is guilty he should be punished," Dr. Rush said.

"If he is guilty," she said pointedly.

"Don't think me presumptuous," the young man said unhappily, "but I care for you deeply. I'm concerned for your safety."

She could tell that his words were sincere and they warmed her. She said, "I'm glad to have someone who cares, a protector. But I'm almost certain you're mistaken in seeing my husband as the Ripper."

"Then why not his father or his brother? One of them must be guilty!"

"Simply because the murders have taken place near Willowgate? No, I don't think that is enough."

They had reached the entrance gates of Willowgate and so the discussion ended between them. At least she now knew what was going on in the young doctor's mind.

It was still raining a little as they descended from the carriage.

As they walked to the entrance, she said, "Thank you for a most interesting evening!"

The young man seemed flustered. "I hope that it wasn't too much of a disappointment."

She looked up at him very directly as they stood in the reception hall of the old mansion. "No. I'm sure that I have gained by it!"

They said good-night and she went on up the shadowed stairway to the second floor and the apartment which she and her husband shared. Once she was alone all the tensions of the night pressed in on her. The fears which had long been dormant returned to plague her and the questions which had not been answered continued to torment her.

She hesitated a moment before she turned the white marble knob of the door leading to the parlor entrance of the apartment. The old mansion was cloaked in an eerie silence. Slowly she opened the door and went inside. The lamps were on and she saw her husband standing at the other side of the room and looking rather weary.

He came across to greet her with a questioning smile on his handsome, Byronic face. "So you went to the theater?"

"Yes, Dr. Rush claimed he'd received your permission to take me."

"That is so," her husband agreed. "But I thought you might have changed your plans because of the wet night."

"It wasn't that stormy. I wore my cloak."

"I see you did," Terence said with a smile. "Let me help you take it off." And he assisted her in removing the crimson cloak. "I like it. It suits you."

"Thank you," she said. "Have you been waiting for me long?"

"No. I was late at the hospital. Taking notes on a brain case. I imagine Dr. Rush explained that to you."

"He did."

They moved on into the bedroom and her husband carefully hung the cloak in the closet where it was kept. Then he turned to her and said, "Tell me about the play."

She stood there frozen with embarrassment. Faintly, she said, "It was thrilling! Very well acted."

Her husband's handsome face revealed a smile. "Come now! That isn't enough! If I allow you to attend the play with that good-looking rogue of a Rush, I at least must get some of the pleasure of it secondhand."

Susan bit her lip. "It wasn't all that enjoyable a play. It was very melodramatic."

Terence was facing her and in his compelling way, asking her, "What was it about?"

She hesitated. "It was a play about murder. About a man with a title who has a second life as an underworld killer."

Her husband's eyes were boring into her. "Indeed?"

"Yes."

"And was the play concerned with finding out he was the murderer?"

She nodded. "Yes. He was caught when he murdered his wife. It had an unhappy ending with his suicide."

Her husband said, "I must say it seems remarkably similar

135

to our classic Jack the Ripper murders."

Susan looked up at his handsome face set in a grim expression now and nodded again uneasily. "Yes. There was a similarity."

"A great one. Did the audience seem aware of this?"

"Yes."

"No doubt that accounts for the success of the play?" he was cold-voiced as he asked her this.

"Possibly," she agreed, aware of his growing tension.

He was studying her with an icy glance. "And what did you make of the play?"

She shrugged. "Not very much. I don't think it proved anything."

"Really? I wonder why Rush took you to such an entertainment?"

"I don't think he knew what the play was about."

"I must ask him a few questions concerning that," her husband said in the same grim way.

"It didn't matter," she said. "I found it a change. Pleasant to see the crowds and be in the theater. We had tea during one of the intermissions."

Terence seemed to relax a little. With a thin smile, he said, "I'm sure it was a profitable evening. Though I promise you I shall question young Dr. Rush about the play the next time he suggests that he accompany you to the theater."

"I'm sure he meant well."

"Of course he did," her husband agreed too easily. "But now I think you should put all thoughts of that play out of your head. You mustn't allow yourself a morbid interest in this Ripper affair."

"I don't want to," she said.

"I have some hot cocoa here," her husband said. "Samantha sent it up to me. My dear sister can be thoughtful at times. And I have saved some of it for you. Take a cup so you'll sleep soundly."

"I don't need it," she protested weakly. "You had better take all of it."

"I wouldn't dream of such a thing," Terence said, bringing her a mug of the warm, creamy liquid. "Drink this down and you'll sleep soundly."

She saw there was nothing to do but humor him. So she took the mug of cocoa and slowly drank it. It was warming and shortly after she began to feel very drowsy indeed. Terence helped her prepare for bed. He even tucked her in carefully as he would a child. Then he bent down and kissed her on the lips. She was gradually losing consciousness as she stared up at him with glazed eyes. And to her horror she saw that in spite of the kiss he'd just bestowed on her the expression on his handsome face was one of hatred. Terrified, she tried to cry out her fear but she was too far gone. Her eyelids closed and she sank into a deep sleep.

Chapter Eight

She awoke to the sound of rain beating against the bedroom windows! It was morning. Her head felt dreadfully heavy and she turned on her pillow to see if Terence was there. But the other side of the bed was empty. It was evident that he'd already risen and dressed. She raised herself on an elbow and gazed about the room as her mind began to work a bit more sharply.

Thoughts of the previous night returned to her. There had been the excursion to the theater and then her confrontation with Terence in the parlor of the apartment. He had not seemed in an especially good mood. There had been a discussion of the play she'd seen and mention of its resemblance to the Jack the Ripper murders. Then he had insisted she take a cup of hot cocoa which had mysteriously triggered a spell of sleepiness in her.

She recalled that Terence had actually helped her undress and had seen her safely in bed. Then there had been his kiss and that last moment when she'd looked up into his face expecting to see love for her written on his handsome features and instead had seen an expression of shocking hatred! She'd been terrified and unable to understand this. And then she'd dropped off into a deep sleep.

The sleep had lasted until the moment of her awaking to the sound of the rain. She badly wanted to talk with Terence and ask him some of the questions troubling her. But she was certain that he must have gone to the hospital by now. He was an early riser and often in the operating room at the hospital by eight. So her questions would have to await his return in the evening. With a tiny sigh she threw back the bedcover and prepared to get up.

Only then did she glance down at her left hand and see the giant ruby ring on her finger. The lovely ring in an ornate yellow gold setting was on the fourth finger of her left hand and she had never set eyes on it before!

She gasped as she stared at it. The ring was obviously a good one and the setting had a rare beauty. But where had it come from? There could only be one answer. Her husband must have placed it on her finger while she slept. He had put it there as a tender token of his love!

Now that she had come to that conclusion she examined the ring more closely. It fitted on her finger well and it was of ancient design and its deep red stone glowed with a savage intensity. Surely it meant that all her fears about Terence must be ill-founded. This was a gesture of a husband who loved her sincerely.

That memory of his face staring down at her with hatred etched on it must have been somehow confused. She must have imagined the look of hatred. Likely it had been her dulled senses that had caused this error on her part. She had fallen asleep almost at once so she'd certainly not been alert.

Unmindful of the bleak day she got up and rang for Sally to bring her morning jug of hot water. Then she went to the window and saw the rain beating down on the lawns, out-buildings, and willow trees of the old estate. It was a gloomy day but the gloom would not tinge her happiness. Terence had gently slid this beautiful ring on her finger as she slept. This act on his part erased many of her fears.

The door from the parlor opened and the yellow-pigtailed Sally came in with the jug of hot water. The maid curtsied. "Good morning, ma'am."

"A very wet morning, Sally," she said, turning to her.

"Yes ma'am," the maid said, pouring some of the hot water from the jug into the china washbowl on the commode which Susan used for her morning ablutions.

She studied the girl with some astonishment and said, "You seem very dejected this morning, Sally."

The maid stood by looking almost frightened. "Yes, ma'am."

"What is it?"

Sally gave her an uneasy look. "The rain began in the middle of the night."

"So?"

"Cook got up to close some of the windows that had been left open," the maid said. "And when she went out to close one in the hall she saw her!"

A ripple of fear went through Susan. "Her?"

The maid nodded solemnly. "Yes, ma'am. The phantom! The first Mrs. Ward what was murdered by the Ripper!"

Susan frowned, much of the feeling of warmth and relaxation leaving her. "You say that the cook claims to have seen Ruth's ghost?"

"Yes, ma'am," the girl said.

"Where?"

"Going up the stairs," the girl said in a frightened tone. "From what the cook says she was wearing her shroud and all just like when she was buried. It fair gave cook a spell! She came running back to her room and woke some of the rest of us up!"

"Did you then go to see the ghost for yourself?"

The maid shook her head. "Not likely! None of us wanted to see it. We were content to take cook's word for it."

Susan's voice was strained, "You shouldn't have listened to a ridiculous story like that. You should have gone and seen for yourselves. I'm sure you would have discovered that the cook was wrong."

"I don't think so, ma'am," Sally said, a determined look on her young, thin face. "Most of use have seen the ghost at one time or another."

All the joy at having received the ruby ring from Terence was being drained away from her. She frowned at the maid. "Well, I don't go along with such nonsense and I don't thank you for bringing me a story like that."

"I'm sorry, ma'am," Sally said, squirming unhappily.

"I shall tell Dr. Ward about it and have him speak to cook," she went on severely. "We can't have such ridiculous stories being told about this house."

The unhappy Sally retreated as soon as she could, leaving Susan to complete her morning toilet and dress on her own, after which she went downstairs to the dining room.

The only one at the table was the stout Phillip Ward, who sat at his place with a dejected air. He made a gesture of rising as she joined him at the table. But it was somewhat like the gesture of an animal in pain. His heart wasn't in it. Then he made a jaded comment on the sort of day it was.

She agreed that the weather was bad and asked if Terence had left for the hospital. She said, "He was gone by the time I awoke."

"Doesn't surprise me," Terence's older brother said. "He leaves for the hospital earlier than anyone else."

"I know," she said.

"I have a bad head," her brother-in-law confessed.

"Too much of that old brandy last night."

Gazing at him across the table, she ventured, "Perhaps you shouldn't drink so much."

His bloated, red face took on a pitiful look. "Now you sound like my wife."

"I'm thinking of your health," she said. "I mean if you really do feel that bad, why drink so much?"

Phillip Ward nodded. "Your comment is well taken. Blame it on my frustration. I always wanted to be a doctor and to this day I have shame feelings for having failed."

"There's no reason why you should have," she said.

"Still, I do," he contended. "Angelica doesn't understand. She thinks as long as I make money in my surgical equipment business it is enough. But it isn't."

The maid came and brought her a dish of hot fish and hashed potatoes. As soon as the maid left the room Susan told Phillip, "There are some nasty stories going the rounds of the servants' quarters once again."

He gazed at her blankly. "Oh?"

"Yes," she said. "Cook claims that she saw Ruth's ghost here last night. On the stairs."

Her brother-in-law groaned. "They're not starting that again!"

"I'm afraid so."

"I thought her ghost was settled," Phillip grumbled. "Now those Jack the Ripper murders are starting once more and we're hearing about her ghost from the servants." He sighed with resignation. "I suppose it is a case of one story starting off the others."

"Then you don't think there's any truth in the story?"

"Of course not! Has to be utter rot!"

"Perhaps, if you spoke to cook you might discourage her from spreading the story," she suggested.

"I shall," he promised. "Just now I must hurry to my office. I have some important customers arriving from the North Country this morning." He got up from the table with a tiny groan and let her finish her breakfast alone.

When she left the dining room she went on to the big

drawing room where she found Angelica seated and reading one of the popular ladies' journals. The blond woman glanced up at her as she entered the room.

"You slept late after your night on the town with Oliver," she said with a hint of a sneer.

Susan saw that her sister-in-law was still suffering from jealousy over the attention the young doctor had shown her. She said, "I've been up for quite a while. I talked with Phillip at the breakfast table."

Angelica arched a shapely eyebrow. "Did you have a wonderful time last night?"

She said, "It was pleasant enough."

"I would have expected it to be something special," the blond woman said cattily. "Not all of us are so privileged as to go out to the theater with a man who is not our husband."

Susan blushed. "You know that Terence gave us permission."

"I can't understand his attitude," Angelica told her.

"He knew it would be a perfectly harmless evening."

"Others might think differently."

"I'm sure my husband doesn't care what others think," she said with a hint of anger. "Terence loves me and trusts me. Look at the beautiful gift he gave me last night." She held out her hand proudly.

Angelica's reaction was not exactly what she'd expected. The blond woman stared at the ruby ring with open dismay and then cried out, "Where did you get that?"

"Terence slipped it on my finger last night," she said, puzzled by the way her sister-in-law was behaving.

The blond woman stood up. "Are you sure?"

"Yes. He did it while I was asleep. When I woke up this morning I found the ring on my finger, I expect he did it that way to surprise me."

Angelica had gone pale. In a low voice she murmured, "It can't be!"

She frowned. "What is wrong?"

Just then the gaunt Samantha came into the room wearing another of her high-necked black dresses and with her hands clasped before her. Angelica, who seemed to be in a state of complete astonishment, turned to the grim Samantha.

Angelica said, "Look at that ring!" She pointed to the ruby.

Samantha did so and it was her turn to register shock. She stared at the ring and gave Susan a frightened look. "Where did it come from?"

"Terence gave it to me!" she said.

"No!" Samantha said in a startled voice. "I will not believe that. You must have gotten it somewhere else."

"No. It came from Terence. I'm sure of it," Susan said.

Samantha looked on the verge of collapsing. In a trembling voice she declared, "You have to be wrong!" And she turned and fled the parlor.

Angelica said, "Well! No wonder she's shocked!"

"What does it mean?" Susan asked.

Angelica stood gazing at her in silence. The rain outside was the only sound between them. Then slowly the blond woman seemed to pull herself together.

She said, "Do you know where I last saw that ring?"

"No."

Angelica looked grim. "On Ruth's finger."

It was her turn to be shocked. "On Ruth's finger?" she echoed in a startled voice.

The blonde nodded grimly. "That's right."

Remembering the bouquet of violets, Susan asked her, "Don't tell me the ring was on her finger when she was buried?"

"You mean like the violets?"

"Yes."

"No," Angelica said with a note of irony in her voice. "It wasn't on her finger when she was buried. And for a very good reason."

She couldn't imagine what her sister-in-law was getting at. She asked, "What reason?"

"You remember that Ruth is supposed to have been killed by Jack the Ripper?"

"Yes."

The other girl paused slightly for effect and then she told her, "It was a particularly gory murder. And among the things the Ripper did was lop off the finger with that ring on it. Neither the ring nor the severed finger was found with the body."

Susan listened with growing dismay. It was worse than anything she could have imagined. In an awed fashion she gazed at the giant ruby and asked, "Then how did it get on my finger?"

"That's something I'd like to know," the blond young woman said wryly.

Susan's attitude toward the ring changed at once. She gazed at it with a mixture of puzzlement and repugnance. She said, "You have to be wrong!"

Angelica was coldly adamant. "I know the setting. I'd recognize it anywhere!"

All the joy which the ring had brought her had ebbed away, leaving her filled only with despair. All she could say was, "No! Terence wouldn't do such a thing to me!"

The blond woman gave her a strange glance. "What makes you think the ring came from Terence? You didn't see him put it on your finger, did you?"

"No!"

"Well, then?"

"How else could it have gotten there?" she asked weakly.

Angelica shrugged. "Anyone's guess will do! My own would be that Ruth's ghost came and slipped the ring on your finger while you were sleeping."

The thought brought her close to panic. "No!"

"Why not?" Angelica's tone was grimly triumphant. "Explain it any other way if you can."

Susan stood there in a turmoil. Then she cried, "You have to be mistaken! It's another ring. Perhaps one like Ruth wore but not the same ring. Probably Terence sought out a replica of the missing ring to give me."

"I'm positive that ring was one of a kind," Angelica's reply. "Terence had it especially made up for Ruth."

"Then he must have had this one commissioned for me," she declared.

"I doubt that," the blonde said scornfully. "He wouldn't want another similar ring to remind him of Ruth and what happened."

There was a frightening logic in her sister-in-law's words. The happiness which she'd known in the ring fell away from her and left her bereft. She recalled the cook's story of the ghost having been seen. Could it be that Ruth's phantom had come to the bedroom and placed this ring on her finger as she slept?

In a broken voice, she said, "I'm sure my husband will be able to explain it."

"I hope so," Angelica said with cold triumph. "But I very much doubt it!"

Susan looked at her with frightened eyes. "How do I know you aren't making this all up to scare me?"

Angelica shook her head. "No. You saw the way Samantha reacted to the ring. She couldn't even remain in the room."

"I'll talk to Terence about it," she said bleakly and she

turned and hurried out of the parlor and up the stairway to her own apartment.

The first thing she did when she got there was to frantically draw the ring from her finger. She studied it and saw there were no markings on it except a jeweler's crest on the inside. Standing there with the ring on the palm of her hand she debated what to do with it. She didn't want to wear it and she wanted to show it to her husband when he returned from the hospital.

With trembling hands she unlocked her jewelry chest and put the ring in one of the velvet storage spaces in it. Then she locked the chest again and placed the key in her pocket. She tried to comfort herself with the thought that Terence would have a perfectly logical and satisfactory explanation for the appearance of the ring but she was by no means sure that this would be true.

The rain dwindled to occasional showers but the day remained bleak. A shaken Susan kept to her room for most of the time, trying to persuade herself there was nothing to worry about, that Terence would be able to explain and everything would be all right. She was seated in an easy chair in her own parlor when a knock came on the door.

"Come in," she called out.

The door opened and it was Sally, the young maid with the yellow pigtails. The girl came into the room with an envelope in her hand.

"This came from next door," Sally told her.

"Next door?" Susan asked, rising from the chair.

"Yes. From Dr. Farrow's sister," Sally said. "Her maid brought it over just now."

"Thank you," Susan said, taking the envelope from the girl. She couldn't imagine what would be in it or why the eccentric sister of Dr. Donald Farrow would suddenly decide to get in touch with her.

As soon as Sally left the room Susan tore the envelope open and extracted the single sheet of notepaper from it. Written in a shaky hand was the message:

Dear Mrs. Ward,
> Will you kindly do me the favor of having tea with me at four?

> Sincerely,
> Agnes Farrow

This was a new and unexpected development. Susan had heard about the strange, retiring sister of the famous surgeon who refused to leave her home or even entertain guests. And she wondered what her sudden interest might be in her? At the same time she realized that there was only one way to find out. Accept the eccentric old woman's invitation. It would also help to take her mind from the worrisome business of the ruby ring.

She dressed and put on her crimson rain cloak and left her apartment. But she'd gone no further than the corridor outside when a figure came hurrying along toward her in the shadows. At first she was apprehensive and then she saw that it was the elderly manservant, Baker.

The gray-haired Baker nodded apologetically to her. "I'm sorry to bother you, Mrs. Ward, but the master is in a very low mood today and he's been asking for you."

She said, "I was just on my way out to pay a call on a neighbor."

"If you could spare him just a few minutes before you go it would be most gracious of you," Baker said. "He needs the sight of a pretty face."

Susan hesitated. "If I went up there I could only stay a few minutes. Otherwise I'd be late for my call."

"Just a few words exchanged with him, would be enough," Baker promised her. "You needn't stay."

"Very well," she said.

"Thank you, Mrs. Ward," Baker said gratefully. "I'll show you the way."

She followed him back along the dark corridor and up two flights of stairs. When they reached the attic level Baker opened a door which led into a large room with several smaller rooms off it. Stretched out on a bed in the far corner of the large room was the ailing Dr. Simon Ward.

She went over to him and gazing down at his bearded face and emaciated old body she said, "Baker said you wanted to see me."

The once famous surgeon stared up at her for a moment as if he didn't recognize her. Then he said, "Yes. You are Terence's new wife."

"That is right," she agreed.

His glazed old eyes studied her worriedly. "I wanted to talk to you. Last night I had a bad dream."

"Oh?"

"Yes," the old man said. "I dream very little. But when I do I have learned that my dreams nearly always have a meaning."

"Please go on," she said.

He swallowed and stared at her. "Last night I dreamed that you were walking across the lawn here and Jack the Ripper attacked you."

She felt herself tense. "What a horrible dream!" she exclaimed. "You must have been thinking of Ruth and what happened to her. Nearly everyone agrees it was the Ripper who murdered her."

"It wasn't Ruth I saw in my dream," the old man argued. "It was you!"

Susan stood there feeling shaken and confused. "I don't know what to say! After all, it was only a dream!"

The old man raised a scrawny hand in warning. "Remember that I told you my dreams nearly always seem to come true. You must be careful! Don't go out alone at night!"

"I seldom ever do," she said.

"You could be in grave danger," Dr. Simon Ward said. Then he shut his eyes and no longer seemed aware of her presence.

She felt a gentle tug on her arm and turned to look into the benign face of Baker. The old servant gave her a knowing nod and she let him lead her out of the attic apartment.

When they reached the head of the stairs Baker told her, "He'll rest more comfortable now. The dream was bothering him. But you mustn't allow it to worry you, ma'am. Just an old man's mad fancies, if you know what I mean."

"He seemed very upset by it," she said nervously.

Baker sighed. "It doesn't take much to upset him these days. But you shouldn't take anything he said seriously. Poor Dr. Ward is no longer himself."

She left the elderly servant standing there by the door of the apartment as she continued on downstairs. In spite of what Baker said the account of the old man's dream had made a vivid impression on her and she determined to be especially cautious about leaving the house after dark.

Now she went out into the gray drizzle of the wet afternoon and carefully crossed to the willow trees and the hedge beyond them which gave access to the Tudor house of Dr. Donald Farrow next door. She picked her steps along the path which led through the thicker grass of the Farrow lawn until she reached the front door of the house.

She lifted the brass knocker and rapped to announce her arrival. After a slight delay she heard footsteps from inside and the door was opened by a prim, middle-aged woman in a maid's black uniform with white apron and cap.

Susan said, "I'm Mrs. Ward. Miss Farrow invited me for tea."

"Yes, Mrs. Ward," the woman said pleasantly. "You're expected. If you'll follow me."

Susan entered the house and trailed the maid down a dark hall. At the end of the hall the maid opened a door on the right. "Go in, Mrs. Ward," she said.

Susan obeyed her and entered the room. At first she was surprised to find it in total darkness except for two candles set out on a table. By the faint glow of their flickering tongues she was able to make out a few details of the room.

Seated very straight in a high-backed chair next to the table with the candles was a thin woman with a stern face which showed a strong resemblance to that of her brother, Dr. Donald Farrow. But Agnes Farrow's face was deathly pale and almost emaciated. The elderly woman wore a dark dress with a high white collar and lace jabot.

In a thin, reedy voice, she said, "So good of you to come, Mrs. Ward. I am Agnes Farrow." And she held out a thin, limp hand.

"I'm happy to meet you, Miss Farrow," she said. "I know your brother."

"Yes," the woman in the chair said. "He has spoken of you. Do please be seated."

Susan sat in a plain chair opposite the old woman. She now saw that the room was furnished like a parlor and that all the drapes were drawn to give the impression of its being night. She said, "You prefer candlelight?"

Agnes Farrow showed a thin smile on her pale face. "I

have no choice, my dear. I suffer from a sensitivity to sunlight. I am deathly ill whenever I'm subjected to daylight."

"How awful for you!"

"It is a nuisance," the older woman agreed. "But I have learned to live with my disability. The great trouble is that most people don't know of my condition and think it strange that I live the way I do. That is why I am setting you right at the start."

Susan was amazed. "Don't you ever go outside?"

"A few times I have ventured out after dark," Agnes Farrow confided in her. "But mostly I am content to remain safely in this house."

"You are fortunate to have your brother," Susan said.

The old woman nodded. "Yes. I am greatly dependent on Donald. I would not know what to do without him."

"I can well understand that," she said. "You are from America?"

"Yes.

Agnes Farrow said, "I have read much about your country. I have always felt I would like to visit it. But, alas, that is not to be."

"I'm sorry," she said. "Is there no hope for your condition? Nothing the doctors can do for you?"

"My brother has brought some of the most famous medical men here and none have been able to do anything for me," Agnes Farrow said. "I will live out the rest of my life in near darkness."

The door of the room opened and the maid brought in a tray and set it out on the table between the two flickering candles. The tray contained cups and saucers in a Crown Derby pattern and a gleaming silver teapot. There was a plate of cakes and one of tiny sandwiches.

"If you will forgive me," Agnes Farrow said, "I'll allow

Martha to pour. My hands are not as steady as they once were."

Martha poured their tea and then left them alone. The old woman sipped from her teacup and after a brief interval, said, "I suppose you are wondering why I invited you here?"

"It makes no difference," Susan said. "I know you must be lonely and I'm happy to pay you a call. I'll gladly come again."

Agnes Farrow's pale face showed gratitude. "That is good of you, my dear. But there was a special purpose in my inviting you here today, aside from my natural desire for company."

"Really?" Susan said, suddenly experiencing some nervousness again.

"Yes," the old woman said, her sunken blue eyes fixed on her. "I'm sure you must be very much in love with Terence to have left America and come the long way here to live with him and his family."

"I'm very much in love with my husband," she said, wondering what this might be leading to.

"Ruth, his first wife, was very much in love with him also."

"I don't doubt that."

"I know it," Agnes Farrow assured her. "I was a close friend of Ruth's. She came here often to visit me. Her death was a great loss to me. Not to mention the tragic fashion in which it occurred."

Susan said, "I can understand that you would miss her."

The old woman looked solemn. "I want to warn you that for a long while Ruth was frightened. Frightened that she might be murdered."

"She told you that?" Susan gasped.

"In so many words," Agnes Farrow said. "I was naturally very distressed."

"Did she tell you what or who she was frightened of?"

"Yes," the old woman said. "She was afraid of becoming a victim of Jack the Ripper."

The words had a startling effect on Susan. In a tense voice, she inquired, "And did she have any idea of the identity of Jack the Ripper?"

"Yes. That was why she was so frightened."

"Did she tell you whom she suspected?"

The old woman sitting there in the faint glow of the candles nodded. "Yes, she did."

"And his name?"

"Her brother-in-law, Phillip Ward," the old woman said.

"Phillip!" she gasped.

"Yes. Do you find it so hard to believe?"

"In a way, no," she said. "Though I would be inclined to suspect the father rather than the son. Dr. Simon Ward is plainly mad these days. I've thought of him as possibly being the Ripper."

"Not likely," the old woman said. "Ruth had sound reasons for her fears."

"Please tell me," she begged her.

"Once she overheard a wild quarrel between Phillip and his wife. He accused Angelica of being unfaithful with the young doctor living there, Dr. John Morley. According to Ruth he tried to attack his wife with a scalpel. Only John Morley's interference saved a tragedy from taking place."

Susan listened tensely. "And Ruth felt that Phillip might be playing the role of Jack the Ripper?"

"She was almost sure of it. And she was trying to gather enough information about him to prove her case. I think that is why he made the decision to kill her. To prevent her from exposing him."

"He does have a knowledge of surgery and the instruments to use," Susan agreed, as she debated the possibility of Phillip's guilt.

"And he is a drinker and weak morally," the old woman said in her stern fashion. "I think he will murder again. I'm warning you because I don't want Terence to lose another wife to his mad brother."

Susan said, "But this is all conjecture. You had only Ruth's suspicions to go on. And she was killed before she was able to really prove anything."

Agnes Farrow said, "I'm satisfied that she was right."

"But you can't be sure," she protested.

"It had to be someone at Willowgate," the old woman in the high-backed chair insisted. "I think the old man is out of the running. He is too weak and elderly, however mad he may be. So you only have Phillip and Terence left. Would you rather suspect your husband than his brother?"

"I don't want to think my husband guilty," she was quick to say.

"Of course you don't. So that leaves only Phillip!"

Susan frowned. "But the murderer needn't have been anyone living at Willowgate. He may be living somewhere nearby. The Wards are not the only medical family in the area."

"They are the most likely to be guilty," Agnes Farrow said. "Consider this. Don't try to jump to conclusions."

"I refuse to do that," she said. "Several strange things have happened at Willowgate."

"I know," the old woman said. "That fall you had. My brother told me about it. I notice you have your arm out of splints."

"Just in the last two days," Susan said. "I still favor it. It's weak from not being used."

"Naturally," Agnes Farrow said. "There is not much happening around here which I don't know about soon after. Your fall and your broken arm were reported to me. I may not be able to leave this house but I have some excellent agents gathering information for me."

"You continue to amaze me," Susan said.

The old woman said, "And then I have another remarkable ally!"

"Oh?"

"Yes. The murdered woman," Agnes Farrow said quite calmly. "Ruth's ghost regularly appears. Last night she showed herself on both the grounds here and at Willowgate!"

Chapter Nine

Susan stared at the old woman seated by the table with the two flickering candles. In the glow of the candles' wavering flames Agnes Farrow's pale face showed an eerie, elated expression as if the thought of Ruth's ghost appearing gave her some strong satisfaction.

Susan said, "I have heard the servants at Willowgate speak of seeing the ghost, but I hardly expected to hear such a statement from you!"

"Why not?" the old woman asked.

"Surely you are above that sort of superstition and ignorance," Susan protested. At the same time she remembered her own encounters with the phantom and the accident which had left her with a broken arm. In an effort to shake this woman's story she was being hypocritical herself. For she had seen the phantom.

"None of us can deny the supernatural." Agnes Farrow said in her reedy voice as she studied Susan evenly. "I am not ashamed to say that I believe in ghosts or that I have seen Ruth's phantom figure in her burial shroud. And whenever I have seen her ghost it has been the sign of some tragic event. That is why I summoned you here today after seeing her last night."

She could not avoid being impressed by the seriousness of the old woman's tone. In a taut voice, she said, "Has Ruth's ghost communicated with you? I mean, has she actually spoken with you?"

"No," Agnes Farrow said. "I have seen her only at a distance but it is a sign."

"I see," she said.

"You may believe me or not," the old woman said. "I've merely tried to be of some help to you. Be very careful in that old house and especially wary of Phillip Ward."

Susan said, "I shall consider what you've told me."

Agnes Farrow studied her with an air of sadness. "It is too bad you married Terence and came this long distance. You know he was a very sick man after Ruth's death?"

"Yes."

"And you still decided to marry him?"

"I didn't learn about his illness until after our marriage," Susan admitted. "But it would have made no difference. I would have married him just the same."

"Would you have?" the old woman seemed doubtful.

"Yes," she said. "If there is nothing else you have to tell me I should go. I'm expecting Terence home soon and I like to be there to greet him."

"What a dutiful wife you are," Agnes Farrow said with a grim smile on her abnormally pale face. "I have nothing more to say. You will either benefit by what I've told you or you'll ignore it. It is entirely up to you."

"I understand," she said. "Thank you."

The old woman made a disparaging gesture with her right hand. "I have done very little. But my warning you at least leaves my conscience clear."

Susan bade Agnes Farrow good afternoon and left the dark room. The maid was waiting in the corridor to show her to the door and Susan had the feeling the woman didn't approve of her or of her visit.

The rain had almost ended and as she picked her way through the grass overgrown path leading back to the hedges she debated it all. The fragrance of the wet trees and the garden filled her nostrils as she approached Willowgate. Agnes Farrow had only served to worry her more.

There was no sign of a carriage or a coachman about and she couldn't tell whether Terence had returned or not or if Phillip or young Dr. Oliver Rush had come home early. On impulse she ventured on into the large, high-ceilinged drawing room. Its shadowed magnificence was hushed with an almost funereal air and there was no one in the room.

Still the same impulse made her walk slowly down the length of the room until she came to the fireplace and the full-length portrait of the late Ruth above. An icy chill raced down her spine as she stared up at the lovely Ruth and her eyes fixed on the hands of Terence's first wife. On the fourth finger of the left hand the artist had faithfully reproduced the striking ruby ring!

She was fascinated by this sight of the ring and was able to identify the one she'd found on her own finger as being the same in appearance. This bore out the weird story of the ring and finger of the murdered girl having been lopped off by her attacker. And somehow last night the ring had found its way to her finger!

Susan forced herself to leave the painting and the living room. She made her way upstairs to the apartment she shared with Terence, her mind whirling with dozens of baffling questions. Entering the parlor of the suite she was surprised to find her husband had arrived home ahead of her and was standing in the center of the room to greet her.

She said, "You're home early!"

He nodded, a satisfied smile on his Byronic features. "Once in a long while I get away from the hospital sooner than usual."

She went to him and kissed him. He held her in his arms for a brief moment. She told him, "I'm glad you're here!"

There was a rather odd, almost ominous glint in his eyes as he asked her, "And where have you been?"

"Next door," she said. "At the Farrows' place."

His eyebrows raised. "Indeed? May I ask why?"

She was growing increasingly surprised at his manner. In a somewhat flustered tone, she said, "I was invited over for tea by Dr. Farrow's sister."

"Agnes Farrow had you over there?"

"Yes," she said, her pretty face shadowed. "And why not? You are behaving as if I'd done something wrong."

His tone was cold steel. "It is quite possible you may have," he said.

She gazed at him with disbelief. This was a Terence Ward she had never known before. "Please explain yourself," she demanded of him.

His handsome face was grim. "Agnes Farrow is an eccentric recluse and a troublemaker. She did all she could to cause trouble between Ruth and me. I do not want you to associate with her."

"You gave me no hint of this before!"

"Because I had not supposed you'd go over there without consulting me," he said coldly. "Why did she have you there? What sort of monstrous lies did she tell you?"

"She treated me to tea and had very little to say," she told her husband.

His eyes bore into her. "I know you are not telling me the full truth. I know the sort of lies she told my first wife. What did she say to you about me?"

"Nothing," she said quite truthfully, since it was his brother whom the old lady had accused. Susan was trembling under this inquisition.

"Did she mention Ruth's murder? Discuss the identity of Jack the Ripper?" Terence's eyes were blazing.

"I don't remember every word!"

"Try!" he insisted, gripping her roughly by the arm.

She looked up at him with tears brimming in her frightened eyes. "She did speak about Ruth. And she thinks she has seen her ghost. She also speculated as to whether Phillip might be Jack the Ripper or not!"

"She accused my brother of that!"

"Because of some things Ruth told her. It seems that Phillip once threatened Angelica with a scalpel. That he behaved like a madman in a jealous fit over the doctor who was living here."

Terence's face was livid with rage. "I knew she must have told you something like that. The woman is mad! She sits there in her dark room and imagines things! I'm sure Ruth never told her anything of the sort. If so she would have mentioned the same things to me and she didn't."

"You're hurting my arm!" she told him.

"I'm sorry," he said and he let her go as a good deal of his anger seemed to drain away from him. He went on, "Donald Farrow is my associate at the hospital and I respect him as a fine surgeon but I also know he is somewhat of an eccentric. His sister is worse; you might even call her mad. The two live a strange life over there. I don't want you to take any part in it."

"Dr. Farrow comes here and is accepted socially by all of you," she said, defending herself.

"That is rather different," her husband said. "I am sorry for him and he is, as I've stated before, a professional associate. So I've extended myself in having him here. But that is the limit of it. I do not want you going over there."

"You should have made that clear," she said.

"I trust is is clear now?"

"Yes," she said. She wondered what he would have to say if he knew that Dr. Farrow had told her about the drug addiction which had sent him to a hospital and ultimately caused the deaths of his two younger associates. Surely that would make him more furious than ever. She was glad she hadn't mentioned this.

In an easier mood her husband said, "Let us put the whole thing out of our minds. I'm sorry I became so upset but I'm weary from my duties at the hospital."

"You left very early this morning."

"I did," he agreed, smiling at her. "But I promise you I gave you a kiss before I went. You were still sleeping so soundly you did not know it."

She frowned slightly. "That cocoa you gave me turned out to be a potent sleeping draught."

"So much the better," he said. "You had an exciting evening at the theater with Dr. Rush and the drink settled your nerves."

Susan said, "I have another strange, thing to tell you and I must beg you before I begin not to become angered."

His handsome face clouded a fraction. "Angered about what?"

"When I awoke this morning I found a beautiful ruby ring on my finger. I assumed it to be a gift from you. That you'd slipped it on my finger while I slept."

He was staring at her. "A ruby ring?"

"Yes."

"I gave you no such ring," he said.

"Then someone else placed it on my finger," she said. Her eyes were solemn. "Both Angelica and Samantha recognized it as being a ring identical to one worn by Ruth at the time of her murder."

"They identified it?"

"Yes," she went on grimly. "According to Angelica the murderer cut Ruth's finger off and the ring vanished with it.

The ring which I discovered on my own finger this morning."

"That's a ridiculous story!"

"I know Ruth did wear such a ring," she insisted. "It is shown on her hand in the portrait in the drawing room. I came from looking at it just now."

This seemed to take him aback. He stood there thunderstruck. Then he said, "There are rings and rings! I'm sure the two cannot have been the same!"

"I will show you," she said. And she left him to enter the bedroom and cross to her jewel case on the dresser.

He followed her, saying, "I cannot encourage your belief in these supposedly supernatural happenings!"

"You will have to accept the evidence of your own eyes," she said. And with a feeling of confidence she unlocked the case and opened it. Then she reached for the ring in the compartment in which she'd placed it and suddenly halted with a gasp.

Standing at her elbow, her husband asked, "What is it?"

"I don't understand," she said in a puzzled tone as she took the ring from the compartment. "The ring I put in here was a ruby with an elegant gold setting. This is a garnet in a tawdry, cheap ring."

Terence took it from her and studied it. "Colored glass," he said with disgust. "Ruth never owned a ring like this!"

Her eyes were wide with disbelief. "I swear this is not the ring which I found on my finger."

Her husband said, "You put it in the jewel box and locked it away. How could it not be the same ring?"

"Someone must have a duplicate key to the box."

"I doubt that."

"They must have! They have come up here and opened the box and substituted this cheap ring for the one I put there originally."

"You asked me to accept the evidence of my own eyes," Terence reminded her. "That is what I'm doing. If someone placed this cheap ring on your finger while you slept it must have been done as a prank."

Tears of frustration came to her eyes. "You won't believe me?"

"In this instance I fear that I cannot," her husband said. "It is time for you to dress for dinner and go down and join the others."

There was a finality in his tone which stopped her from trying to argue with him further. She knew he had decided against her and he would not budge in his views. Nor would it do any good to try to drag Angelica or Samantha into it as a witness since from her other experience with them she could only expect them to join against her. She could only accept the humiliation and wait for a chance to prove her story.

By the time they arrived downstairs Phillip Ward was already in a fairly drunken state. Angelica was standing by her stout husband regarding him with a cold look of disgust. Samantha sat apart from them with a glass of sherry in her hand and young Dr. Oliver Rush was standing near the door waiting to greet them.

Terence smiled at the younger doctor and said, "I owe you a debt. My wife tells me she thoroughly enjoyed the theater in your company last night."

"It was my great pleasure," Dr. Rush said politely.

Terence went on, "Though I must say that I consider your choice of play somewhat unappetizing. Could you not find a better entertainment than one based on the career of Jack the Ripper?"

The young doctor's pleasant face crimsoned. "I did not know the subject of the play until after it began."

"In that case I'd say you were most negligent," was her

husband's observation. "But since Susan enjoyed herself we shall say no more about it."

Terence then crossed to the sideboard to prepare himself a drink, leaving her alone with the young doctor for a moment. She said apologetically, "You mustn't mind my husband. I didn't resent the subject of the play. In fact it gave me food for thought."

Dr. Rush gave her a meaningful look. "I have an idea that was what the playwright had in mind."

"I'm certain of it."

He said, "I trust I didn't cause you any unpleasantness with the doctor?"

"No. You mustn't worry."

He looked upset. "I feel responsible for you in this. Please tell me if Dr. Ward resented our going out. I can't imagine why he should since he gave me permission to invite you."

Now Terence came back to interrupt their conversation. He gave her the usual glass of sherry and sipped his own whiskey and soda as he told Dr. Rush, "I plan to have you assist me in a delicate brain operation in the morning. Dr. Farrow is coming to dinner tonight and we shall discuss it later. He will also be involved."

"Thank you, sir," the young doctor said, obviously excited at the prospect of being assistant at the important operation.

Terence then began to discuss hospital matters with him and Susan moved on to join the drunken Phillip and his lovely blond wife, Angelica. Phillip was bleary-eyed and standing there none too steadily. It wasn't hard to picture him as a weak character who might deal in murder furtively under the cover of darkness and in the guise of a legendary character like Jack the Ripper. Had Ruth been right in her suspicions, as Agnes Farrow seemed to believe? And had she finally been murdered because she'd come to know too much?

Phillip offered Susan a drunken smile. "Hear you passed an evening watching Jack the Ripper on stage," he said.

"I think the play was based on his character," she agreed.

"Holds all of London in terror," Phillip said. "There's a fellow who really knows how to wield a surgeon's scalpel!"

"Something you were never able to do!" his wife said with a sneer.

Phillip turned to the blond Angelica with drunken dignity. "You don't know what you're talking about!"

"And I'm sure that you do!" Angelica retorted. "Or perhaps it is the whiskey which is forming your sentences."

Phillip chose to ignore his wife and again turned unsteadily to Susan. He said, "As you may have observed since joining our little group here, the marriage between Angelica and myself is not exactly a love match! Nor was it made in heaven! Rather the other place, if one considers. And beyond everything my wife does not understand me. She continually underrates me! Do you believe that?"

Susan was saved the embarrassment of having to answer this by the appearance in the room of the stern Dr. Donald Farrow. The older surgeon bowed to her husband and the others gathered in the drawing room and then came directly to her.

Smiling, he said, "I believe you had tea with Agnes today?"

"Yes."

"Most kind of you," he said. "You know she is shut off by herself a great deal because of her health condition."

"She explained that to me."

The stern man beamed on her. "So she appreciates company when it is available and of the sort she enjoys. She was most enthusiastic in her praise of you."

"That was very kind of her," she said, keenly aware that

her husband had drawn near them and was listening to their every word.

Dr. Farrow said, "You must not be a stranger in our house. I urge you to visit Agnes again. See her as often as you can."

"I shall try," she said carefully, avoiding any definite promise since she knew Terence was there to hear her and he had given her strict orders not to visit the elderly woman in the future.

Now Terence spoke up with a sort of false heartiness and said, "We've been awaiting your arrival, Farrow. Samantha has a prime roast beef waiting for us which we musn't let spoil. I'll get you a whiskey and we'll go straight in to dinner."

Susan had no more opportunity to chat with either Dr. Farrow or the young Dr. Rush alone. Her husband kept close by her for the balance of the evening. Phillip retired from the group early pleading a headache, though he was plainly drunk. After he left Angelica lavished her attention on young Dr. Rush. It was evident that she was determined to keep him as an admirer even though he'd taken Susan to the theater. Watching it all Susan found it grimly amusing.

At last the social evening ended. Dr. Farrow offered his thanks and said good-night to them all. As soon as he left, young Dr. Rush excused himself since he would have to be at the operating table early in the morning. The evening had been a kind of ordeal for Susan. Her remembrance of the unhappy quarrel between herself and Terence over her visit to Agnes Farrow still upset her and she was also tormented by the weird business of the ruby ring.

Terence accompanied her up to their apartment seeming his old self again. He was full of charm with none of the harshness he'd revealed earlier. Being with him in this mood almost lulled her into a feeling of security. Almost! Not quite!

Long after they were in bed she gazed up into the shadows of the big bedroom with troubled eyes and tried to decide what the day's events had really meant. She was still occupied with this when her eyes closed and she gave way to a weary sleep.

When she woke it was still dark. She thought she heard footsteps in the corridor outside and then distant voices in an agitated mood. She turned to ask Terence about these things and to her shock and dismay found that he was no longer in bed with her.

She raised herself up in bed and realized her heart was pounding more rapidly than it should. Again she heard a distant voice cry out downstairs. She knew she could no longer remain in bed. Finding her robe she threw it around her and then hurried across to the door and opened it.

A figure came down the dark hallway and as it drew near she recognized it as Baker in a shabby bathrobe. She asked him, "What is wrong?"

"Nothing now, ma'am," the old servant said. "A while ago I found the old doctor had slipped away on me! I was fair upset! But it's all right now. We've got him back and safely upstairs again."

Susan felt a surge of relief. "So that was it!"

"Yes, ma'am," the old servant said, the tufts of his white hair standing comically up on end. "I'm afraid we made a bit of a racket."

"It doesn't matter. Just so long as the old man is safe."

"He's fine now," Baker said. "Tonight he had one of his vague spells and I should have been on guard. But you forget."

"I understand," she said. "My husband helped you find him, I suppose."

Baker stared at her. "Dr. Terence?"

"Yes."

168

"No, ma'am," the old servant said. "To be truthful I haven't seen him nor Mr. Phillip. Though young Dr. Rush did join us in the search and finally found him walking out on the main roadway."

She listened with a sinking heart. All the relaxation she'd felt left her. In a tight voice, she said, "You're sure my husband didn't join in the search?"

"Quite sure."

"I don't understand it."

"What is wrong, ma'am?" Baker asked anxiously.

"My husband is out somewhere. He's neither in his bed nor in the apartment."

Baker stood there confused. "I can't think where he might be."

"Nor can I," she said. "Will you kindly check for me?"

"I will, ma'am," the old servant promised. And he went back down the corridor.

She stood in the doorway of the apartment in a shocked state. It was a repeat of the strange absences of her husband before. Apparently it was to start again. The first thing that came into her mind was his cocaine addiction. Was he still a slave to the drug? Was that why he so frequently vanished in the middle of the night?

She went back into the parlor of the apartment and lit one of the lamps there. Then she began pacing up and down nervously as she waited for some word from Baker. She had an eerie feeling that she was on the brink of some dire tragedy. It was a premonition she could not shake off.

After a little Baker returned to tell her apologetically, "I'm sorry, ma'am, but I haven't been able to locate Dr. Terence."

"It's all right, Baker," she said wearily. "Go to bed. You must be exhausted."

She went to her own bed but she did not sleep. Perhaps an

hour later she heard footsteps from the parlor and then Terence came into the bedroom. He was fully clothed and had a haggard look.

He stared down at her. "You're awake?"

"Yes."

"When did you find out I was missing?"

"Quite a long while ago," she said. "Your father managed to escape and I was wakened by the efforts to catch him and bring him back."

"I see," her husband said quietly. "I suppose you are curious as to where I was?"

"What do you think?" she said, bitterly.

"I'm sorry. I didn't know you'd wake up before I returned. I had to go out."

"Why?"

He hesitated. "I needed something."

She sat up in bed. "Terry, I think I know."

"What?" he eyed her warily.

"I know what's behind these sudden disappearances of yours," she said. "It's drugs."

He reacted to this as if she'd touched him with a red-hot poker. "Drugs!" he echoed.

"Yes," she said soberly. "Dr. Farrow told me about your tragic addiction and illness soon after I arrived here. I've known for a long while."

Terence was very white. He sat down at the foot of her bed and held his head in his hands for a moment. He spoke without looking at her directly. "I didn't want you to ever learn about it."

"I was bound to. Why didn't you tell me yourself?"

He dropped his hands and looked at her now and she saw his despair. "You can never have respect for me again!"

"You're wrong about that," she told him. "Dr. Farrow

explained how your addiction had come about through medical experiments. You have nothing to be ashamed of. You have fought to free yourself of the drug."

"If you only knew how I have fought," he said, reaching out to take one of her hands in his.

"I believe you."

His eyes met hers earnestly. "Every so often, when I've been under great strain, I have returned to the drug. I refuse to have any of it near me as a temptation. So tonight, as on those other nights, I went out in search of it."

Susan said, "I have every confidence in you. I know that one day you will have no need of it."

"That will be all the more true because of your belief," her husband assured her.

They talked until dawn began to show at the windows. Then he left her to shave and have some food before going to the hospital for the early morning session of surgery which had prompted him to go out seeking cocaine in the middle of the night.

Susan returned to sleep for a while. When she finally woke the sun was shining in through her window and she knew it was later than her usual hour of rising. She quickly got up and pulled the bell cord to summon Sally with the usual jug of hot water for her morning toilet. But Sally did not come with the water with her customary promptness.

As a result Susan washed in cold water. Even after she had dressed there was still no sign of Sally though she'd rung the bell cord several times. She couldn't imagine what might have happened unless the girl with the yellow pigtails was ill. In that case someone else should have answered her call.

Concerned about this she left her room and made her way downstairs to encounter a troubled-looking Samantha standing in the reception hall.

Susan went down and asked Terence's older sister, "Have you any idea where Sally is? I rang for her but she didn't answer."

The gaunt-faced Samantha said, "We're looking for her now. She's missing. It seems she is nowhere in the house."

"Missing?"

The prim woman in black nervously twisted her thin hands. "Yes. Phillip has remained here to lead the search. Her bed was not slept in last night and we fear there has been foul play."

"Oh, no!" she said with a tiny moan and felt she might faint.

Samantha gave her an apprehensive glance. "Are you all right?"

"Yes," she said faintly, although this was far from the truth.

"You had better go get your breakfast," the thin woman said. "It is hard to tell how long it may be before we have any word of the girl."

"She was a nice child. Surely nothing dreadful has happened to her," Susan said. "Do her parents live nearby? It may be that she decided to spend the night with them."

"We tried her parents and they haven't seen her," Samantha said.

She stood there for a few minutes longer and then went on to the dining room, though she could not think of having anything more than some hot tea. She entered the long, darkish room to find Angelica still seated there alone.

"Good morning," the blond woman greeted her. "Have you heard the news?"

"Yes. I'm shocked!"

"No need to be yet," Angelica told her. "She'll likely turn up safely. She's of an age now to interest men. The chances are one of them talked her into running off with him."

Susan sat at the table and asked the maid for tea. She was still upset, despite Angelica's more cheerful prediction that Sally would turn up safely.

She said, "I don't see Sally as the kind of girl who would do that."

"Don't you believe it," the blond young woman said. "I know these servant girls. They are all alike."

Susan gave her an impatient frown. "I don't consider that either a true or fair statement."

The coldly lovely Angelica shrugged. "You may have your opinion and I'll have mine!"

Susan sipped some of the hot tea and felt better. Then she asked the blond woman, "Is Phillip taking charge of the search for her?"

Angelica smiled in her mocking fashion. "As well as he can take charge of anything. He insisted on staying home from business and playing the role of squire. I doubt if the girl will ever be found with my husband organizing things."

She would have liked to be able to contradict Angelica on this but found it impossible to do so. She asked her, "How is he feeling this morning?"

"Badly. After drinking the way he did last night he had to feel badly this morning."

"Terence left for the hospital early with Dr. Rush," she said. "So I don't imagine either of them will have heard about this."

"Not likely. You know that old Dr. Ward escaped for a while last night?"

"Yes. I was wakened by their efforts to get him back upstairs," she said. "It seems to have been a night for things to happen."

Angelica gave her a direct look. "I wonder if he might

know anything about the girl?"

Susan put down her cup. "You mean? . . ."

"He's not altogether in his right mind," Angelica said. "If he met her out in the darkness it's hard to say what might happen."

"Don't say such things!" Susan protested.

"It's possible."

"Dr. Ward is a fine old man despite his senility," Susan insisted. But at the same time she was worrying about what he'd said to her. He'd talked to her about a strange dream he'd had in which she'd been attacked by the monster, Jack the Ripper. Had these been imaginings of a sick mind rather than a dream? And might he have tried to act the Ripper role out?

Angelica was studying her with hard eyes. "You're just as worried about what he may have done as I am," she said. "That old man should have been placed in an asylum for the insane a year or two ago."

"His sons couldn't do that. He was a famous surgeon. He started the hospital where Terence works now!"

"That is all past him," Angelica said coldly. "I've tried to reason with Phillip. But he is weak and allowed Terence to sway him. So the old man has remained here. And now we may be faced with a true scandal!"

Susan got up, unwilling to listen to any more such talk. It was bad enough to find themselves in this predicament without Angelica suggesting such dire things. She was also worried by the recollection that Terence had left the house in the middle of the night and gone off somewhere for drugs. He had returned in a drug-sustained state. Was it possible that he might have been responsible for some crime during that time?

Fortunately Angelica knew nothing of Terence being absent. But Susan knew she'd told Baker so sooner or later this truth would come out and it might make for some embarrassing questions for both herself and Terence.

Susan went back out to the reception hall just in time to see Phillip Ward enter the house. The stout man looked to be in a shaken state. He stood before her and Samantha for a moment without speaking, but with a look of horror on his bloated face.

Samantha asked him sharply, "Well?"

He shook his head grimly. "We've found her. She's dead. Murdered! Looks like Jack the Ripper again!"

Chapter Ten

The words of the stout man spelled out Susan's worst fears. She stood in the background feeling the room swirl around her. For a moment she was sure she was going to faint. She reached out a hand to touch the wall and steady herself. Then as the first impact of the tragic news subsided she gradually regained some control of herself.

She heard Samantha ask, "Where is the body?"

"Under the willow trees on the other side of the boundary line between Farrow's property and ours," Phillip Ward said. "We missed it first time around."

Samantha said, "Then she must have been on her way to the Farrows or coming back from there."

"She was certainly over there unless whoever killed her deliberately took the body to that spot. And that doesn't seem likely."

The prim woman asked in a taut voice, "You think it was the Ripper? Was she badly mutilated?"

The mustached face of the stout man showed a kind of greenish shade. He shook his head again. "I'd rather not think about it or talk about it. Whoever it was cut her up properly. I'd say it was Jack the Ripper again!"

"Have you sent for the police?" the spinster asked.

"A carriage is on the way with the word now," Phillip said.

"What about the body?"

"We covered it with some canvas. We wouldn't want to move it until the police come."

"No," Samantha agreed. "Of course not. Poor Sally! So we are to go through all that awful business of a police investigation again!"

Susan took a step forward to address the two. She said, "Terence ought to be told."

Phillip blinked at her. He seemed to be still suffering from a severe hangover. He said, "Yes, I guess he should."

"He and Dr. Rush left very early for the hospital," Samantha remembered.

"Yes," Susan said. "They had an important operation to take care of this morning. Dr. Farrow was going to be assisting in the surgery as well."

"That means his sister is there alone," Samantha said. "She also should be told. It wouldn't be fair to wait until the police arrive and burst in on her. She's not in good health."

"I agree she should be told," Susan said. She turned to Phillip and suggested, "You'd better send another of the servants to the hospital to leave word for Terence. You can put vital details down in a short note. And I'll undertake to go and inform Agnes Farrow since I met her yesterday."

"Very well," Phillip said. "I'll write the note at once and have someone take it."

Samantha gave her a questioning look. "You're sure you don't mind going over there?"

"No," she said. "I'll avoid the spot where the body is. And it will keep me occupied. I can't bear to just sit around and think about it."

At this moment Angelica joined the group. She took one look at them all and said, "You needn't tell me. You've found her and she's been murdered!"

Phillip stared at her bewildered. "How could you possibly know that?"

"I read it in your faces," his blond wife said. And then she went over to him to have him give her the details of the murder.

Susan went upstairs to get her cloak. When she reached the closet she opened the door and found that it was missing. And only then did she remember that the unfortunate Sally had been very fond of the crimson all-weather cloak. She'd even found the maid trying it on when she'd entered the bedroom unexpectedly one day. A cold streak of fear shot through her as she began to suspect that Sally must have borrowed the cloak for her midnight tryst.

She quickly found another cape and went downstairs again. Phillip and the two women were still there talking quietly. She went up to him and asked, "Did you notice what Sally had on? Was she wearing a cloak of any kind?"

The stout man frowned and said, "Yes. She had on a crimson cloak. Very much like the one you sometimes wear."

"It was my cloak," she said. "I tried to find it just now and it's missing."

"How dare she take your clothes!" Samantha said, outraged.

"I wouldn't worry about that now," Susan said with irony. "But I did want to know if she had the cloak."

"I'm afraid it won't be much use to you again," Phillip warned her. "It's badly torn by the knife that fellow used and bloodstained as well."

"It doesn't matter," she said. "Don't forget to get that note to Terence."

"I won't," he promised.

She told them, "I'm going to Agnes Farrow's now. If you want me before I return you'll know where I am."

She left the three waiting for the police. A small knot of workmen from both the estates had gathered around the spot where Sally's body had been found. She avoided going near this area of the lawn and made directly for the entrance of the old Tudor house. She knew that her husband might be angry at her visiting Agnes Farrow again but she didn't feel that important under the circumstances.

She was thinking about Sally in that crimson cloak which everyone identified with her. And the chilling thought struck her that Sally's murderer might have mistaken the maid for her. Wearing that cloak could have sealed the girl's death warrant. It could be that whoever had murdered the girl had intended to murder her!

If the killer had been Jack the Ripper, then she had been added to his list of prospective victims for some reason. Her mind was working quickly. She recalled that the woman she was now on her way to visit had claimed that Ruth believed Phillip Ward to be Jack the Ripper.

Yet just now Phillip had reported this murder with the air of a thoroughly frightened man. It seemed impossible that he could have coldly committed the crime on the one hand and then nervously reported it on the other. Yet she knew such things were possible. There were lunatic criminals possessed of dual personalities. The crime committed by the violent personality often offended and shocked the more normal side of the dual individual's character. So perhaps Phillip could even yet be suspected of this atrocious deed.

Even more terrifying for her was the possibility that her own husband had been involved. Surely he had been out of the house at the time of the murder and he'd been taking cocaine. Could he have had a spell of madness under the drug in which he'd killed poor Sally? Worse still, had he attacked the girl thinking it was she! He might have been enraged at the thought she was following him and had learned the secret of his addiction.

Reaching the door of the Farrow house she knocked and

waited to be let in. In the long interval before the door was answered she also thought about the part old Dr. Simon Ward might have played in the tragedy. He had been missing for a while last night. Had he somehow found a scalpel and attacked the girl in his madness? It was another disturbing possibility.

The Farrow maid let her in and took her up to the bedroom occupied by the elderly Agnes Farrow. The invalid was still in bed in the darkened room with a lamp giving off the only light. She at once asked Susan, "What has happened out there?"

"One of our maids was murdered last night," she said. "The body was found on your lawn."

The pale woman's face registered distress. "Dear me! So it is all to begin again!"

"I'm afraid so. I thought I ought to let you know."

"That was good of you," Agnes said gratefully. "Of course the police have been sent for."

"Yes."

"And my brother should be told."

"I have arranged to have a message sent to the hospital," Susan said.

"Thank you."

"No doubt my husband and your brother will return as soon as they can."

"I hope so," Agnes Farrow sighed. "I'm not well enough to deal with the police." She gave Susan a knowing look. "I told you that I had seen Ruth's ghost and another tragedy was soon to take place."

"I believe you did."

The invalid gazed at her solemnly from her bed. "Ruth showed herself to me as a warning."

"It seems the murder is typical of a Jack the Ripper

killing," Susan said.

"So the monster who killed Ruth and those other unfortunates has struck again!" Agnes said. "You know that Ruth suspected your brother-in-law, Phillip!"

"I can't seem to fit him in the picture," Susan said. "He led the search for the body and he appeared very upset by the discovery of it."

"He could be pretending," the elderly Agnes Farrow said.

"Perhaps."

"You must be doubly careful from now on."

"I know," Susan said grimly. "That girl was wearing a cloak of mine when she was murdered. I'm not sure but that I was the intended victim and she was killed only by mistake."

The invalid stared at her. "You think that?"

"I can't help worrying about it."

"Let us pray the police will bring that monster to justice this time," Agnes said indignantly. "Queen Victoria wrote a strong letter to *The Times* about the fiend still being at large. She is as upset as the rest of us."

"Not that it does much good," she said.

"Be thankful it's not you out there dead on the grass rather than that poor girl," Agnes Farrow said.

"I must go back now," she told the invalid. "I felt you ought to hear the facts from one of us. If you need us for anything don't hesitate to call on us."

"Thank you," Agnes Farrow said. "You're a dear child and I shall tell my brother so."

Susan left the invalid's dark bedroom with a sense of escape. She felt that Agnes Farrow had been doomed to a most unhappy existence by her sensitivity to sunlight. The woman was a virtual prisoner of her condition. Stepping out of the grim Tudor mansion into the morning sunshine made her feel somewhat better.

But there was truly no feeling better on a morning which offered this sort of tragedy. She hastily made her way back to Willowgate, arriving just a few minutes before the police came on the scene. She remained inside, peering out the front window of the drawing room as Phillip guided the officers to the body and went through the business of stating the details of his discovery of Sally's mangled corpse.

Both Angelica and Samantha watched from other rooms. In a little while the police would come to question them. But none of those in the house would have much to offer. Susan was still staring out the window when she heard someone coming into the drawing room.

Turning she saw that it was the elderly Dr. Simon Ward. She went to him, since she was the nearest, and said, "Dr. Ward, you oughtn't to be down here!"

The old man with the long white hair and white beard gave her an impatient glance. "Why not? This is my home!"

"I mean it's a bad time for you to be here," she said.

"Any time seems to be a bad time as far as all of you are concerned," was the old man's bitter reply. "I understand a murder has been committed and I've come down to find out about it."

She told him the victim was Sally and begged him, "Go back to your apartment until the police leave."

"I have no fear of being questioned," the old man said. "You will remember that I told you Jack the Ripper attacked you in one of my dreams."

"I do."

"I can see into the future," he boasted. "I was wrong about his victim. But I did foretell the killing!"

"Don't say anything like that to the police," she warned the old man.

"Why not? It is a gift of which I'm proud!"

"They'll think you mad and maybe charge you with the murder," she warned him. "Don't you understand that? You were out of the house last night. You had the opportunity to do it!"

The bearded former surgeon eyed her with derision. "My mind was not on murder. I was enjoying the beauties of nature. The myriad of stars overhead and the peace which had descended over the estate with the coming of darkness!"

"And all the while a murder was being committed!"

The old man pointed a skinny forefinger at her in a trembling gesture. "I do not want you telling me such things. I have no interest in them."

"You may hear it from worse people than I," she warned him. "The police will not be considerate when they come to question you!"

"I shall say nothing!" the old man informed her grandly. And with this said, he turned and strode out of the room to vanish somewhere in the rambling big house.

She was relieved to see him go. And it was only a few minutes later when the inspector in charge of the case came to interrogate all of them. He had the odd name of Wayland Ragsdale.

A nervous Phillip Ward made the requisite introductions but the inspector seemed to know most of the company from his being there at the time of Ruth's murder. He was a rather remarkable character, a stout man wearing a flashy brown check suit and a deerstalker cap. He had a round, intelligent face with prominent gray eyebrows and heavy side-whiskers of the same hue. When he doffed his cap he was revealed to be bald except for a fringe of gray hair.

He seemed particularly interested in her. Coming up to her the massive man said, "So you are the new Mrs. Ward?"

"Yes," she said. He towered a full head over her.

"You have recently come here from America, I understand," he said in the resonant voice one would expect from a man of his wide girth.

"That is so."

"Too bad to have you involved in such a distressing event," he said. "But no doubt you had heard of your predecessor's violent death at the hands of Jack the Ripper?"

"Not until I came to England," she said.

Inspector Ragsdale looked surprised. "Dr. Ward didn't inform you of his first wife's fate?"

"It is something he hates to talk about."

The big man made a gesture. "But surely he would discuss it with you."

"Only when he found it unavoidable," she said.

"Interesting," the inspector said. "I believe this girl was wearing your cloak when she was murdered."

"Yes."

"Fortunate for you that you weren't in it," he said.

"Yes," she agreed in a faint voice.

His sharp gray eyes studied her for a moment. Then he said, "I shall have some other questions to ask you later." He turned to Phillip Ward and told him, "Just now I'd like to speak to your father. Will you direct me to the old gentleman?"

"Yes," Phillip said nervously. "I believe he is upstairs. Isn't that so, Samantha?"

Samantha nodded. "He went back up to his rooms a few minutes ago." She gave the inspector a pleading glance. "I trust you won't bother him too much, Inspector Ragsdale. He is very confused these days and easily upset."

"I promise to be as tactful as possible," the inspector said with a grave nod.

The three of them went upstairs with Phillip leading the

way and Samantha and the inspector following. Susan found herself alone in the company of the blond Angelica.

Angelica waited until the three were out of earshot before she said, "That Inspector Ragsdale is no fool."

"I would think not," she agreed.

"He thinks one of us killed Sally."

Her eyes widened. "You really believe that?"

"Yes," Angelica said grimly. "He thought the same thing when Ruth was murdered. That the killer was in this house. And because both that murder and this one bear the mark of Jack the Ripper he has an idea that a lunatic surgical murderer lives under this roof. He'll leave no stone unturned to prove this. To catch Jack the Ripper would make him the hero of all England."

"Because there are doctors living here doesn't mean the murderer has to be one of them. There are other doctors in the area. Dr. Farrow, for instance."

Angelica came close to her and in a conspiratorial tone said, "You're surely aware that he selected you for special questioning."

She tried to maintain calm. "No doubt that's because he didn't meet me when he was here before."

The blond girl smiled grimly. "It wasn't you he was interested in. Those questions were meant to reveal things about Terence and his attitude toward you!"

"Terence!"

"Yes," Angelica said spitefully. "You may as well realize that it is your husband whom he suspects of the murders and of being Jack the Ripper."

"No!" she protested, panic rising up in her.

"Better to face it. The crimes began again on Terence's return to England. And according to Baker you were looking for him last night at the hour the murder must have taken place! He had left your bedroom in the middle of the night!"

Susan felt sick. She had known this would come out but she'd not been aware that the word had already spread. She said weakly, "The fact he wasn't in the house doesn't make him a murderer."

"It certainly makes him a suspect!" Angelica snapped back.

"So is his father a suspect! He escaped last night! It was Baker bringing him back that woke me up."

The blond girl sneered. "That poor old man is hardly as likely a murderer as your husband."

"What about your husband?" she demanded, thinking of what Ruth had told Agnes Farrow. "He has crude surgical knowledge. He could be the Ripper!"

"He went to bed drunk and slept through everything until I woke him!" the blond girl said with malicious triumph.

Susan turned and hurried from the room. She fled up the stairs to her own apartment to escape the cruel baiting of her sister-in-law. She knew that Angelica had always hated her and now in this crisis she was viciously turning on her. It seemed the blond girl could not get over losing Terence and now she wanted to see him destroyed rather than happily married to anyone else.

She remained in the apartment to escape the drama going on in the old mansion. Several times she went to the window and gazed out at the spot where the body had been found. Once she was just in time to see the funeral carriage driven in and the body of the dead girl carried on a stretcher and placed in it. The massive Inspector Ragsdale supervised the body's removal.

It was still hard to think of Sally as dead. And more difficult to think of any motive for her slaying other than mistaken identity. This meant that she had been the intended victim.

Now she waited for the return of her doctor husband so that she might tell him all that had happened and warn him that a web of circumstantial evidence was being spun around him. He was very likely to be accused of the killing.

Angelica had made this seem very certain although Susan had entertained fears of her own prior to the acid exchange with the blond wife of Phillip. Angelica had been most positive that her husband had slept through the night. But did she have to be telling the truth? She might be lying to protect the weak Phillip. This started a new train of thought in Susan's mind and she was still pursuing it when she heard a carriage in the driveway and looked out to see that her husband and Dr. Oliver Rush had returned.

Rather than go downstairs where there was bound to be a good deal of talk and confusion she decided to wait in their apartment for him to join her. The minutes went by, testing her patience, but she had decided on a course of action and she was not about to change it. She guessed that her husband was being questioned by Inspector Ragsdale and that he would come to her as soon as he could.

It was a full fifteen minutes later before the door of the parlor opened and a worn-looking Terence came in. He shut the door and stared at her with a completely shattered look on his handsome face.

She went to greet him, "My poor darling!" she said.

He came to her and took her in his arms and held her to him closely. In a low voice, he said, "What a horrible business! Poor Sally!"

She drew back to ask him, "Did the inspector talk to you?"

"Yes."

"What did he ask?"

He shook his head wearily. "I can't begin to tell you. All kinds of questions."

"Did he question Dr. Rush and Dr. Farrow?"

"He asked Rush only a few questions. He didn't seem all that much interested in him. He's gone over to see Farrow now."

"I see," she said with a sigh. "It's obvious he doesn't suspect Dr. Rush."

"Why should he?"

She looked up at her husband's handsome yet haggard face with frightened eyes. "This is the second Jack the Ripper murder to strike this household. He's looking for a suspect among us."

Her husband showed alarm. "You think so?"

"I'm sure of it," she said. She hesitated, before she asked him, "Does the inspector know that you have been a cocaine addict?"

Terence frowned. "Yes. That came out when Ruth was murdered. But what has that to do with it?"

"It makes you more suspect," she said worriedly. "You are at once more apt to be guilty in his eyes."

"Nonsense!" Terence said. "I am the only one who has suffered from my use of the drug. I have never been violent because of my addiction."

"I doubt if he'll believe that," she warned him. "And everyone seems to know you left the house last night."

Her doctor husband ran a hand through his curly, black hair. "That still doesn't make me a killer."

"They'll find out where you went and why," she said. "When they know it was to get that drug they'll think you killed her under its influence."

"I didn't want the drug to excite me," he argued. "I needed it to calm me down. I had that important surgery to do this morning. Operating with the aid of cocaine has become such a habit with me I felt I needed it just this once more. That was why I went out to find it."

"I believe you," she said. "I only hope they do."

He began to pace up and down restlessly. "You're probably right. Ragsdale was very curt with me. I wouldn't be surprised to have him come back at any time and charge me with the murder."

"He's looking for a criminal with surgical knowledge and you fit the bill," she said bitterly.

"So he decides I'm Jack the Ripper," Terence said, halting and standing there with a grim expression as if he realized his predicament fully for the first time.

"Something like that."

"But I had nothing to do with it!"

"I know," she said, unhappily. "Let us hope the truth will come out and we can prove it."

Her doctor husband sighed. "I feel it is something I can't fight. Inspector Ragsdale will have to do his worst. I have a patient at the hospital I must return to. The operation this morning seemed a success. But the patient needs my constant attention through the first critical hours following the surgery. I should be there now. I ought never to have left him."

"You had to come here."

He sighed. "Mostly because of you. Otherwise I'd have let the inspector seek me out there. Now I must drive back."

"I'll be in terror every moment I'm here alone," she said.

"You mustn't allow yourself to feel like that," he told her. "I expect more courage from you."

"I'll try."

"And you'll be a credit to me," he said. "I'll return from the hospital when I safely can. It may not be for hours and it may not even be tonight. It all depends on my patient."

With this final word he kissed her and left. She remained in the apartment in a state of near panic. She heard his carriage draw up and then move away and she had never felt so very much alone.

The afternoon passed and Samantha had a plate of food sent up to her since she'd signified she would not go down to dinner. She had no appetite and was only able to take a little of the food.

Dusk began to settle and the melancholy of the blue twilight well suited her mood of despair. She felt as if she were caught in a trap and that her doctor husband shared the same fate. It seemed that a snare of guilt was tightening around them and they could do nothing about it.

She was seated by the window with the room almost in darkness as she had not lighted any of the lamps in the parlor or bedroom. Sally had always looked after this chore and now Sally was dead. Suddenly there was a light knock on the door. The unexpected sound sent a tremor of fear through her. She at once regretted not having any light in the room.

Getting up from her chair she moved hesitantly toward the door and in a frightened voice, asked, "Who is it?"

"Oliver Rush," came from the other side of the door in the young doctor's familiar voice.

Her fear left her. She went to the door and opened it. She said, "You're back from the hospital! What about Terence?"

"He's still there," the young doctor said, coming in and closing the door after him. "The patient is hovering between life and death and he cannot leave him just yet."

"I'm so frightened," she said.

"My poor Susan," the young doctor said and he took her in his arms and gently kissed her on the forehead. "You know that I am at your command. I'll do anything I can to help you."

She looked up at him through the shadows and smiled gently. "Dear Oliver! You are such a good friend!"

"I feel very helpless just now," he said unhappily. He let her go and turned away from her slightly. "I'm sure you have come to realize that I'm deeply in love with you."

"And I care for you, more than I ever believed possible," she told him. "But I have a husband. You understand that as well as I do. The most there can ever be for us is a warm friendship."

Oliver turned to her impulsively. "You say you have a husband. But I wonder."

"Wonder what?"

"Is he truly all that you think him? Or is he something quite different!"

She stared at the young man with dismay. "I can't think that you are deserting Terence along with the others!"

"I'm thinking of you," he said as they stood there in the darkness facing each other. "I'm becoming afraid for you. I respect Terence as a doctor. I think he's a genius. But I'm not at all sure that he isn't also a little mad!"

"You mustn't think that!"

"I know Inspector Ragsdale suspects him!"

"That shouldn't shake your belief in him! You know him so much better!"

"I want to be loyal to him," Oliver said in a despairing voice, "but there is a great deal of evidence pointing to him."

"Not really!"

"There is!" the young doctor insisted. "There is a pattern to these Jack the Ripper murders. And the pattern indicates that the killer has surgical skill and a hatred of certain types of women. Terence's first wife was a victim of the Ripper and I think the victim last night was meant to be you. The cloak fooled him. That is why Inspector Ragsdale is so sure that Terence is his man!"

"There are others. Why not suspect the old doctor or

Phillip, or you or Dr. Farrow?"

The young man standing opposite her in the dark seemed struck by this statement on her part. In a grim tone of resignation he acknowledged, "You are right! Your husband is not the only suspect."

"We must remember that," she urged him.

The young doctor said, "Still I'm far from convinced of his innocence. He brought you here without telling you the truth about his first wife's death and he has subjected you to the same dangers."

"I know," Susan agreed unhappily. "I have had my moments when I've felt distrust of him. But I want to believe he had nothing to do with these murders."

"The police have established that the Ripper is a doctor and probably one living in this area," Dr. Rush said. "That does narrow down the suspects considerably."

"I would like to talk to Dr. Farrow," she said. "I wonder if he has returned to the hospital with Terence?"

"I think so," the young man said. "They are both much interested in the brain case which they operated on this morning. They talked of returning to continue their observations of the patient."

"And you?"

"I'm the minor member of the team," the young doctor said with a hint of bitterness. "Just as I appear to be playing a minor role in your life."

She went near him again and touched his arm gently. "That is not true. I regard you as my best friend."

He said, "I can only hope when all this is cleared up that I may aspire to another relationship with you."

Susan knew that he was saying he believed Terence to be the monster, Jack the Ripper, and that he was counting on his being charged and convicted of the murder of Ruth and the others. She could understand the young man's feelings but she was not yet ready to agree with him.

She said, "You must go now. I'm weary. I think I shall retire even though Terence has not returned."

"Is there anything I can do to make you more at ease?" the young doctor asked.

"Help me light the lamps," she said.

"At once," he told her and he set about lighting the lamp in the parlor and the one on her bedside table in the bedroom. When he finished, he asked her, "Will you feel less afraid now?"

"I will," she said with a faint smile. "There is just one other favor. I feel I could do with a glass of sherry and there is none here in the apartment. Could you bring me up a glass?"

"Of course," he said, his serious face full of concern for her. "I'll be back in a few minutes."

He left the room to take care of the errand for her and she stood thoughtfully by the fireplace of the parlor wondering how it was all going to end. She found herself in a frightening dilemma. There was so much evidence to indicate that Terence might be the multiple murderer wanted by the authorities and yet he had protested his innocence to her. Had he been lying?

She was weary of the suspense and doubts. It seemed years rather than months since those days of their happy courtship in America. The darkness had truly descended on them with their return to England. She had known small respite from fear since the first night in London when she'd wakened to find Terence absent from their bedroom. And on that very night the Jack the Ripper killings had been resumed.

Surely she was fortunate to have a male friend like Dr. Rush, who had made it clear that he would even like to marry her if she were free. Her thoughts were interrupted by a soft knock on the living room door. Expecting that the young doctor had returned with her glass of sherry she opened the door quickly.

But to her extreme horror it was not Dr. Oliver Rush who stood there in the shadows but the phantom figure of the murdered Ruth, wearing the shroud in which she'd been buried!

Chapter Eleven

Before the horror-stricken Susan could make any outcry the
shrouded figure burst in on her and seized her with powerful
hands. The stench of the grave filled her nostrils as the
clawlike hands tightened around her throat. By the time she
attempted to scream for help all she could manage was a
hoarse, gasping sound.

The ruined face of Ruth's corpse loomed over her in
the struggle. She could barely make out the decaying
features through the netting of the shroud. All the stories
about the haunting of the old mansion returned to her as she
made a last feeble effort to free herself. Then she blacked
out!

When she opened her eyes young Dr. Oliver Rush was
bending over her anxiously. He lifted her up from the floor
and held her in his arms solicitously.

"What happened?" he wanted to know.

"The ghost," she said weakly.

"Ghost?"

"Ruth's ghost! I thought it was you at the door. But it was
a horrible phantom in a shroud! The same one I've seen
before!"

The young doctor was frowning. "Go on," he urged her.

"The phantom attacked me before I could shout for help,"
she said.

"And then?"

"I don't know."

He said, "Whoever it was must have heard me returning.

When I came into the room you were alone and in a faint on the floor."

Susan shut her eyes in remembrance of the horror. "She smelled of the grave!"

The young doctor's tone was grim. "Can you honestly believe you were attacked by a ghost?"

She opened her eyes. "I've seen it before and so have others in the house. Ruth's ghost!"

"I wonder," he said.

At the same time he lifted her up from the floor and carried her into the bedroom and placed her on the bed. Then he fetched the glass of sherry which he'd gone downstairs to find and handed it to her.

She sipped the sherry and felt better for it. "You must have frightened the phantom off," she said.

Young Dr. Rush stood at her bedside with a skeptical expression. "I scared someone away. I'm not sure it was a phantom."

"Who else?"

"That remains to be seen," he said. "You ought to have someone with you for company. Shall I call Angelica?"

"No!" she said at once. "Not Angelica! We don't get along well. She can be very unsympathetic."

"I know that."

"I'll be all right."

"I don't want you to be alone. At least not for a while," he said stubbornly. "I'll find Samantha and bring her up here."

She sighed. "If you feel that you must."

"I do," he said. "I'm responsible for your welfare while your husband is at the hospital. Let us hope he soon returns."

"I hope so," she agreed.

The young doctor left her briefly to go in search of Samantha. That he found her was attested to by her appearance only a short time afterward. The gaunt woman in black slowly entered her bedroom and came to stand at the foot of her bed.

Looking a good deal like an apparition herself in the dim light of the bedroom, Samantha said, "Dr. Rush asked me to come to you."

"I know," she said, sitting up in bed. "But I don't feel it's necessary."

Samantha's gaunt face showed a weird expression. "He said that you'd been attacked by someone."

"Yes."

"Who attacked you?"

She said, "Ruth's ghost! The same phantom I've seen before. Of course Dr. Rush doesn't believe me!"

The thin woman in black curled a thin lip as she said scornfully, "But then he is very young!"

"It was the ghost! I'm sure of it!"

"Ruth cannot rest in her grave as long as Jack the Ripper lives," was Samantha's comment. "She wants to revenge herself upon him."

"But why attack me?"

The gaunt face of Samantha revealed a knowing look. "It may be that she is jealous of you as Terence's second wife. You have taken her place."

"You think that?"

"It is as reasonable an explanation as any," the gaunt woman said.

She considered this and saw that Samantha might be right. She said, "Perhaps so."

"You ought to leave this house before something worse happens to you," the stern woman in black advised her.

"I can't desert my husband now!" she protested.

"Perhaps he'll ask you to leave," Samantha said. "Terence

is living under a dark cloud now."

"Because of Sally's murder?"

"Partly that," Samantha agreed. "And then there is what has happened in the past. Inspector Ragsdale is most suspicious of him."

Susan gazed at the gaunt woman with startled eyes. "Surely you have no doubts about your brother?"

"I no longer know what to think," Samantha said nervously. "Do you want me to remain with you for the night?"

"No," she said, somewhat angered by the woman's lack of loyalty to Terence. "I'm all right now that I've recovered from my shock and I don't expect the ghost will show itself again tonight."

"Probably not," Samantha agreed and a few minutes later she left.

Susan was glad to see her go. While Samantha was not as plainly opposed to her as Angelica, there was resentment there. Susan could feel it. There was a something in Samantha's quiet manner that exuded menace. She could not explain it but she recognized it.

With Terence's older sister out of the room Susan prepared for bed. By the time she was ready to put out the bedside lamp she heard the door of the parlor of the apartment open. Her nerves on edge, she called out, "Who's there?"

To add to her terror there was no immediate reply. She heard the footsteps coming toward the bedroom and a moment later her husband stood before her. Terence looked more weary and shaken than she could ever remember. He stood there in his topcoat and black top at with an expression of defeat on his Byronic face.

Gazing up at him, she asked, "What is it?"

"The patient died," he said dully.

She was at once sympathetic. "I'm so sorry."

"Farrow and I labored all the night to save him but we lost him an hour ago," her surgeon husband said.

"You must expect some defeats," she reminded him.

"This was a major one," Terence said with a deep sigh. "I risked a great deal on the operation."

"Perhaps next time you will succeed," she said in an attempt to cheer him.

He took off his coat and hat and tossed them on a nearby chair in a disgusted gesture. "There may never be another time to try my new method."

"Of course there will be!"

He looked at her blankly. "I doubt it. Time appears to be running out for me swiftly."

His somber mood was new and shocking to her. She had never seen him so resigned to failure. It frightened her since it could be an indication of his guilt.

She said, "Things have been bad but I'm sure they're bound to be better soon."

"I see no sign of it."

"I'm sure you will if you don't give up," she said. She had been going to mention the ghostly attack on her but now she decided against this. She would save it to tell him in the morning. They would both be better able to cope with it then. So she merely urged her husband to make ready for bed and get the rest he so badly needed. For herself, it was enough to have him by her side in this time of terror.

But when she woke up the next morning she had no opportunity to discuss the ghostly attack of the night before with her husband as he had left for the hospital. A new maid, named Jenny, brought up the hot water for her morning toilet.

Jenny was a stocky, talkative girl with auburn hair. She bustled about filling the china basin with hot water and confiding in Susan, "It's a wicked day, ma'am. The fog that thick you could slice it!"

"I see that it is," she agreed, gazing out the window and noting that even the nearby willow trees were blotted out by the curtain of gray mist.

"That's London for you!" Jenny said with a grimace. "I liked the weather a lot better back in Sussex."

"Is that where your home was?"

"Yes, ma'am," the girl said. "I left there two years ago to go in service. There's not much else for a farmer's daughter to do but be a maid. Not unless you marry one of the farm boys and set up in an estate cottage, and I wanted none of that. I saw my poor mother work herself to an early grave as the wife of a tenant farmer!"

Susan listened to the girl's comments and judged that she was a young woman with a mind of her own. She said, "And now you've taken over Sally's job."

"Yes, ma'am," the stocky girl agreed. "But I don't mean to let the same thing happen to me what happened to her."

"Oh?"

"No, ma'am," Jenny said emphatically. "I'm not one to run about with strange men like Sally!"

This was a new side of the late Sally and interested Susan. She asked the girl, "Was Sally a flirt?"

"Of course she was!" Jenny said with an indignant toss of her head.

"I had no idea."

"She was always leading some young man on," the stocky young woman said. "And you see where it led her."

"Have you any idea who she was meeting that night?" she asked, growing more and more interested.

Jenny looked grim. "She wouldn't tell us. But she said it was a real toff! And older than her! Of course she could have been lying. The last gentleman friend she had was the butcher's lad."

"The butcher's lad?" Susan echoed the girl. She was thinking of the cruel way the girl had been mutilated. Perhaps by a surgeon or why not by one skilled with a butcher knife?

"I was questioned by the inspector and I told him all I knew," the stocky girl said proudly. "I think she was meeting some swell and he was the one what did her in."

"A swell?"

"Yes. Maybe some important doctor. Cook thinks maybe it was Dr. Farrow since she was over there."

She gasped. "Dr. Farrow is not that sort of man and he is years older than Sally was."

The maid rolled her eyes knowingly. "Cook says you never can tell about men! And Sally never minded going out with men who were older. She used to laugh and brag about it!"

"I see," she said quietly.

The stocky girl gave her an inquisitive look. "And she was a thief too, from all I hear. Didn't she take your cloak and when they found her dead body she was wearing it?"

Susan reprimanded the girl. "That is something I would prefer not to discuss."

Jenny crimsoned. "Yes, ma'am."

When the maid left her she thought over all that had been said. It was obvious that the latest murder was being discussed freely in the servants' quarters. It was a fresh view to know that Sally had been of a flirtatious nature and apt to lead men on. And it was rather shocking to realize that the good Dr. Farrow could even rank among the suspects.

The house was normally quiet but now when she reached the ground floor she found the atmosphere almost funereal! She had breakfast alone and noted the sober manner of the maid who waited on her. When she finished the meal she went on to the drawing room and stared out the window at the fog. It was as heavy as any she'd seen.

She was standing close by the drapes when she heard someone coming into the room. Pressing against the thick drapes so as not to be seen she watched as the ancient Dr. Simon Ward came slowly hobbling in. He was leaning heavily on a gnarled oak cane and he passed her without even seeing her.

The mad old man continued on down the length of the big, shadowed room to halt before the painting of Ruth above the fireplace. He gazed up at it and began mumbling something to himself in a voice too low for her to hear.

She left her place of concealment by the drapes and quietly followed him down toward the fireplace. When she was only a few feet distant from him she halted and tried to overhear what he was mumbling.

The old man was babbling something about, "Ghost . . . nightly visits and the Ripper!" He seemed greatly agitated.

Susan was suddenly seized with an urgent desire to cough. And before she could stop herself she coughed aloud. It was a signal for the old doctor to wheel around and glare at her with a kind of fury.

"Why are you spying on me?" he demanded angrily.

"I wasn't," she protested.

"I know better," Dr. Simon Ward said threatening her with his walking stick. "You are all working against me! All trying to prove me mad!"

"That was not my purpose, I promise you," she said, taking a step back.

The dark veins at his temples stood out in his anger. His bearded face was contorted with rage. "Ruth was the only one who respected me!" And he moved toward her menacingly.

She said, "I, too, have been your friend."

The old man hesitated and eyed her suspiciously. "You are the new wife. I keep forgetting."

Susan asked him, "Why did you leave the house night before last?"

"To find her."

"Her?"

"Ruth," Dr. Simon Ward said with a mad gleam in his sunken eyes. "You know that her ghost returns here. You must have seen her."

"I think I have," she said cautiously. "At least I've seen some macabre figure in a shroud. Night before last it attacked me!"

The mad old doctor said, "She returns because she wants the truth about her murder to come out."

"There was another murder last night," Susan reminded him. "The servant girl, Sally." She watched him for any reaction to this, thinking that he might reveal if he was the murderer.

He gave her a wily glance. "Sally was murdered?"

"Yes."

"Then it must have been Jack the Ripper again," was his rather disappointing answer. "They ought to catch him!"

She was going to reply to this but Samantha came into the room and, seeing her father there, showed some dismay. The gaunt, dark-clad Samantha went over to the old man and took him gently but firmly by the arm.

"You know you ought not to be down here, Father," she told him.

He looked upset. "This is my home!"

"But you are ill," his daughter placated him. "Some harm might come to you down here. You must let me take you back upstairs."

Dr. Simon Ward became downcast. "You have made me a

prisoner," he said unhappily.

"Only for your own good," Samantha said as she led the old man out of the drawing room.

Susan watched the two go and again wondered if Dr. Simon Ward might not be the murderer they were seeking. He was mad enough and he had the medical knowledge to perpetrate the Jack the Ripper killings. Were all his family banded together in an unholy alliance to protect the old man from the authorities and try to keep him from doing further harm?

If this was true they had not succeeded very well. She was worried that the old man might have killed Sally on his escape from the house the previous night. Thus far there seemed to be no proper explanation of where he'd been. And while she hated to see the mad old man convicted, considering his previous high professional station as a doctor, she knew she'd prefer the father being guilty to the son. The all-important thing was that Terence be innocent and she was unable to be positive about that at the moment.

The London fog continued to remain thick. And she heard from Angelica that burial rites were to be held for Sally early the next morning. The blond woman suggested that it was custom for members of the family at Willowgate to attend such services. The interment was to be in the family cemetery in the rear of the estate, a section shielded from sight by a thick stand of willows. From what Susan learned, a section of the cemetery was given over to those servants who had no family burial plot. It seemed that Sally's family lived a distance away and had requested that the Ward family take care of burial details.

After lunch Susan put on another of her cloaks and went out to see if she might encounter Dr. Donald Farrow on his afternoon stroll. He had informed her that he always took it except on those days when rain threatened. Since the day was marred only by thick fog she assumed he would keep to his regular routine. With this in mind she crossed the lawn and went through the opening in the hedge to the Farrow property.

At first she saw no sign of him and then he appeared out of the gray mist walking toward her. She at once hurried to greet him.

Reaching him, she said, "I was afraid I'd missed you."

The stern-faced man shook his head. "No. I was a little later coming out than usual. My sister Agnes is greatly distressed by this latest tragedy."

"I'm sure she must be," Susan said. "We all are."

Dr. Farrow seemed very tense. "What is the news of the tragedy?"

"None," she said. "No one seems to know anything about the poor girl's murder other than it's believed she was a victim of Jack the Ripper."

"The papers are bound to make a fuss about it," the tall man in his dark tweed suit said gloomily. "And the usual sensation seekers will be coming here to view the spot. We went through it before when Ruth was murdered."

She sighed. "I'm sure you had more than a taste of that sort of unpleasantness then."

"The police were in to question both me and my sister," be went on with a frown. "Did you talk with Inspector Ragsdale?"

"Only briefly," she said.

"He's a strange man. Hard to tell what he is thinking."

"Oh?"

Dr. Farrow gave her a troubled look. "He is familiar with Terence's history of cocaine addiction and because of it I have a feeling he has made up his mind that Terence may be Jack the Ripper."

"It is what I've been fearing," she said. "And I'm sure it's not true. I'd much more quickly blame his father or Phillip. His father escaped from Baker's custody night before last around the time of the murder."

"I heard that," Dr. Farrow agreed. "But I cannot see the old man as our Jack the Ripper. He might commit one pointless murder but never a series of them."

"Whoever killed Sally must have known something of her habits and that she was out at the time. Why do you think she came over here?"

Dr. Farrow's stern face darkened. "As a matter of fact I had a rather nasty argument with Inspector Ragsdale about that. He tried to intimate that she might have been coming to our place. I did not know the girl; neither did my sister. So that is silly!"

Susan suggested, "Perhaps she knew she was being followed. She apparently had been with a young man and after saying good-night to him sensed that she was being trailed. She might have been closer to your house than Willowgate. That could explain her being found on your side of the property line. She may have been trying to reach your door."

The tall man listened to her with interest. "That could be the case," he agreed.

"I had a dreadful experience last night," she said. "And had it not been for Dr. Rush I might have been found dead in my room." And she went on to tell about the shrouded figure attacking her.

Dr. Farrow looked shocked. "What did Terence have to say about it?"

"Nothing," she said. "I haven't told him that it happened."

"You haven't told him?" the stern doctor asked incredulously.

"No. He's so very upset as it is. And last night when he came in he was especially downcast about that patient you'd operated on dying. I planned to wait and tell him about the phantom this morning after he'd had a night's rest. But when I awoke this morning I found he'd gone to the hospital."

"He must be told," Dr. Farrow said.

"I suppose so."

The stern man was emphatic as he said, "There is something very unusual going on at Willowgate. And it begins to seem that you are at the very center of it."

She said grimly, "Terence's sister has suggested the ghost is jealous of me and wants to harm me for that reason."

"I'm not convinced of that," the older doctor said. "My belief is that these ghostly appearances are linked with the Jack the Ripper murders."

"Perhaps the police will discover the truth," she said.

"At the moment I have little faith in that," Dr. Farrow replied. "I'll be seeing Terence at the hospital before you do. May I tell him about this phantom attack on you?"

She hesitated. "If you will explain that I held the truth back from him last night for his good."

"I shall certainly do that."

"Then you may tell him," she said.

Dr. Farrow said, "I think it important that he know. He may soon have to defend himself in the matter of Sally's murder and he should have all the information available about the various happenings here."

They parted on this. Susan went back to Willowgate and was surprised to find Phillip Ward had returned early from his place of business in London and was already well on his way to being drunk. As she entered the reception hall he came out of the drawing room with a filled glass in hand and hailed her.

"Why are you running from me?" he demanded in a slightly slurred voice.

"I'm not."

He stood there swaying with an ugly look on his bloated, purple face. "You can't wait to get upstairs."

"Not really," she said, gazing at him directly. "At first I didn't know you were here. I didn't expect you home so early."

He took a swig from the glass and gave her a disgusted look. "You don't know what it's like having everyone plaguing me about the murder! Asking a lot of silly questions! I had to get away from it!"

"I'm sorry," she said quietly.

"You know you were a fool to leave America and marry my brother?" the stout man said thickly.

Susan was shocked by his statement, feeling that it might have some sinister meaning. She said, "Why do you say that?"

"Because Willowgate and its people are cursed!"

"You sound very sure."

"I know," he said gloomily. "There have been the murders and the phantoms. Terence sought you out and married you because he thought it would change things here. And it hasn't."

She said, "I would hope that he married me because he loved me and that he brought me here because it is his home and he wanted me to share it with him."

The drunken man gave her a knowing look. "Then he should have honestly told you there were other things you'd have to share here! Things to make your flesh creep! Danger that would make you lie awake in the dark with your eyes open in fear!"

Susan felt humiliated since she knew that Terence had not

been honest with her in revealing Ruth's murder by Jack the Ripper or the tales about her phantom haunting Willowgate. Her husband had deceived her from the start, was it possible his deception had been even greater than she'd guessed?

Still she felt the need to defend him against this drunken brother, who might well be the monstrous Jack the Ripper himself. She said, "I think Terence was silent with me about certain things because he wanted to be kind to me."

Phillip Ward stared at her with glazed eyes. "You love him and so you refuse to believe anything evil about him?"

"I'm trying not to," she said. "Is that wrong?"

"No," the stout man said in a sudden change of mood. "Not wrong at all. I only wish I had a wife who held the same faith in me!" And he turned and staggered back into the drawing room to leave her alone.

She mounted the shadowed stairway with a new feeling of desolation. Then she went straight to the apartment she and Terence shared and remained there until he returned from the hospital shortly before the dinner hour. He came into the parlor, where she was standing staring out at the fog.

She managed a small smile of greeting for him. "I was afraid you'd be late. With the fog so thick traffic must be moving slowly."

"And with difficulty," he agreed. "A dray and a stage coach collided in Marston Road and blocked everything for a while. Now a lot of the public vehicles have men walking ahead of them with lighted lanterns. Even at that it is difficult to spot them."

"I'm glad you're back safely."

He kissed her and held her in his arms to study her with gentle eyes. "And so am I. Dr. Farrow told me about your weird encounter last night and I've been greatly worried about you."

"It's only one of a series of such happenings," she said. "Dr. Farrow seems to think the appearance was somehow linked with the murders."

Her husband frowned. "I can't always agree with him."

She gave Terence a concerned look. "He claims that Inspector Ragsdale knows about your battle with cocaine addiction and that because of it the inspector is apt to think you guilty of Sally's murder and perhaps the others."

Her handsome husband looked grim. "Since Farrow has been so frank I think there is something I should tell you. He was also mixed up in that cocaine business."

She gasped. "You can't mean it!"

"He doesn't think I know," Terence said grimly. "But he was experimenting in the company of another surgeon at the same time my assistants and I used the drug to expand our energies."

Susan asked the next question which came to mind. "Do you think he's still taking cocaine?"

"I've been watching him closely," her husband said. "There are a few telltale signs which make me suspect he is an active addict while I have only occasionally taken cocaine in recent months."

She stared at him. "In that case he may not be all that dependable, and yet he has always seemed my best friend."

"It could be he has acted the role well," Terence warned her. "It also could be that under the influence of drugs he may be a completely different person from the Dr. Farrow with whom you've talked."

"Would the police know of his addiction?"

"Not likely," he said, "since it isn't generally known at the hospital. But I note that he's taken care to let the police know that I have been addicted."

Her eyes widened. "You think he has been trying to cast

suspicion on you and protect himself?"

"What could be more natural?"

"I don't know," she lamented. "I can't decide what to think. I've always counted on him so!"

"I'm sorry," her handsome husband said. "I know how badly you need to feel you have friends. But I can no longer hide this truth about Farrow from you. You must keep it in mind."

"I shall."

Dinner that evening proved an ordeal. Phillip was drunken and loud with his wife Angelica being especially resentful and angry in her crosstalk with him. Samantha sat in a kind of dull misery while Terence looked pale and concerned. He and Susan tried to maintain some semblance of a normal conversation without much success.

After dinner Terence took her aside and told her that the undertaker would be bringing Sally's body for burial at ten the following morning. "I shall be present," he said. "And I would appreciate it if you showed up at the graveside."

"It will not be easy for me in my present state of mind," she admitted frankly. "But I'll be there if that is your wish."

"I'm sure it would be appreciated by the other servants," he said. "And Sally was a faithful maid to you."

"I know," she agreed quietly. She was thinking that Sally might have even died in her place because she was wearing that crimson cloak. Someone might have decided the maid was she and so had taken her life.

She and Terence retired early that night. It proved to be a night without event. But the morning was again cloaked with thick fog. It would surely be a grim day for the funeral service. She mentioned this to her husband, who had donned a black suit for the occasion.

He frowned. "It doesn't much matter. The tragedy is that

Sally lies dead in her coffin."

After a frugal breakfast they prepared to leave for the cemetery. Phillip, sober, but looking shaky after his long night of drinking, was on hand and also wearing a black suit. Angelica refused to attend the service and Samantha begged off because of feeling ill. So Susan found herself making the short walk through the foggy morning to the cemetery with the two men. They had kept the news of the funeral from old Dr. Simon Ward and so there had been no problem of dissuading him from being there.

Susan hung on her husband's arm as they made their way toward the willow grove which served as a barrier between the rear of the estate and the family cemetery. The stout Phillip walked along beside them with a frown fixed on his face. She glanced up at Terence and saw only a kind of determination etched on his handsome features. It was hard to tell what he was feeling.

Her own feelings were confused. She had been fond of Sally and it was hard to believe the girl was dead and this was the occasion for her burial. They walked through the open section between the trees and came out at the burial ground. It was not large and it was fenced on four sides with a low iron fence. The burial party had gathered in a far corner of the cemetery and at first could barely be seen through the thick fog.

As Susan and the two men approached the grave she saw the small cluster of servants gathered there to pay their final respects. The white-haired vicar also stood at the head of the grave with his prayer book in hand while the undertaker and his two assistants stood back a small distance. The undertaker's top hat was draped with black crepe.

As soon as they took their places by the grave the vicar began the service. It was a tense occasion, as well as a sad one.

Susan noted that neither Dr. Farrow nor his sister was present. But during the service the burly Inspector Ragsdale and an assistant appeared to stand respectfully with the mourners. Only then did it strike her that the inspector felt that Sally's killer was at her funeral. Present there among them! And in all likelihood he was there to see if her husband might show some betraying emotion to mark him as the murderer.

She gave Terence a troubled glance and saw that his face was unusually pale and that he seemed lost in listening to the words intoned by the old vicar. She let her gaze wander and she was suddenly caught by what seemed a movement in the bushes outside the cemetery fence and across from her. And in the next instant she saw the phantom shrouded face which had haunted her from almost the first moment she set foot in Willowgate!

Chapter Twelve

The gruesome, shrouded face peered at her from the shadows of the bushes for barely a moment and then vanished. The effect on Susan was to make her suddenly go rigid. She barely stopped herself from crying out. Then as the phantom face vanished she looked up quickly to see if Terence or any of the others had noticed it. By their unmoved expressions she decided they had not, that she had been the only one in all the group assembled at the grave who had seen that horror from the bushes.

The vicar ended his service and the undertaker's assistants began to shovel the gravel into the grave. Susan turned away from the open grave and winced a little at the sound of the hard gravel striking the plain wooden coffin. Both Terence and Phillip had gone to confer with the vicar and the undertaker, leaving her alone.

She was standing there in the cold morning fog ignored by everyone when suddenly a burly figure came looming up before her. It was Inspector Ragsdale.

"Good morning, Mrs. Ward," he said in his gruff way. His top hat was still in hand from the service.

"Good morning," she said nervously.

"I would like to have a talk with you," the police inspector said. "I think it might be important to you."

"Oh?" She was a trifle surprised and uneasy.

"But I'd prefer it to take place away from Willowgate," he went on.

"I see."

"There is a pub, the Bull and Bear, not more than three blocks from here if you go straight down the street without making any turns at all. I should say it would take you about ten minutes to walk to it."

"Which direction?"

"Straight past the Farrow house," the inspector said. "I'm very busy at the moment, a half-dozen investigations under way for which I'm responsible. I have little time to spare. Could you meet me at lunch, say around twelve-thirty?"

"I suppose I could," she faltered.

The big man with the gray side-whiskers gave her a severe look. "I mean without allowing any of the others to know about it. That is most important. Do you think you can manage to get away without anyone at Willowgate being the wiser?"

"I guess I can manage it," she said. "I would expect my husband to return to the hospital and his brother to go to his shop as usual."

"Excellent," the bald Inspector Ragsdale said. "I shall be awaiting you at the Bull and Bear at half the hour after twelve." He bowed. "And you will promise to be discreet or I fear naught can come of it."

"I shall try," she promised.

"My assistant will be outside the pub watching for you," the Inspector said. "It is agreed?"

"Yes," she said in a small voice, "I shall be there."

"Thank you, ma'am," the big man said and donned his hat once more.

She stood there in a mild daze wondering whether she had done right as the inspector and his assistant strode away from the graveside rapidly.

As they vanished in the willow trees her husband returned to her side. Looking somewhat upset Terence asked her,

"What did the inspector have to say to you?"

She decided quickly on her reply and said, "He offered me his regrets."

"Strange!" her husband said, glancing after the two police officers as he still held his top hat in hand. "I should have expected him to have offered his condolences to me or to my brother, Phillip."

"He saw that you were both occupied, I suppose," she said. "He claims to have a great many investigations under way and little time."

"Indeed!" Terence said seeming relieved by this word. "I'm not at all sure I like the fellow. His manners leave a lot to be desired."

"I didn't notice. He seemed most polite to me," she said glibly. She was amazed at how easy it had been to lie to her husband and also how easily he had accepted her story.

They started away from the grave in the footsteps of the inspector with Phillip trailing after them with the vicar talking earnestly at his side.

As they walked, Terence asked again, "That fellow made no reference to the crime?"

"No."

"And no mention of Jack the Ripper?"

"None."

"I find that remarkable," her husband said. "The fellow is always prying."

"He wasn't just now," she said carefully, knowing she would surely be in trouble at this point if Terence caught on. "Perhaps it was the occasion."

Her husband's handsome face showed bitterness. "I have rarely known police officials to show sentiment."

"Still they must at times," she insisted. And with a glance

up at him. "Surely you haven't had all that much experience of them?"

Terence was at once a trifle flustered. "You are right," he was quick to agree. "My exposure to the police has been of a most limited nature."

"So I have understood," she said as they came within sight of Willowgate.

As they continued walking Terence said, "I surely hope he has given up the stupid idea that I may be Jack the Ripper."

"Do you think the authorities ever truly thought that?"

"According to a few remarks they let drop before Farrow," he said grimly, "I have been one of their chief suspects. He likely attended the service today to see if I showed any guilty signs at the grave."

"You think so?"

"I fear that was what brought him and that assistant here," her husband said darkly as he came to a halt before the stables. "I must leave you now. I will have a carriage made ready and go to the hospital."

"Then I shall not see you again until this evening?" she said, anxious to have his reassurance that this would be the case.

"No. I won't be back until then," he agreed. "I have a busy day scheduled at the hospital."

"Pray don't be too late," she begged him. "I shall be waiting your return."

"I'll do my best to be early," he promised. "The fog will play some part in it." And he removed his top hat to briefly, yet with great gentleness, place a kiss on her lips.

She stood for a moment as he walked toward the stables, then she turned and made her way to the house. She'd barely gotten inside when Phillip Ward came in as well. He'd apparently said his good-byes to the vicar.

Now he stood staring at her in a rather dazed way with his top hat still on. He announced, "I think I shall get drunk."

She gazed at him wide-eyed. "What good will that do? I'd say it's a poor way to show respect for Sally."

"Whatever you may think," the stout man said, "this is my only means of finding escape from an ugly situation. I shall lock myself in the study and get dead drunk!" And having said this he marched off down the hallway to the study.

Susan frowned as she watched him vanish in the darkness of the hall. She wished that he'd gone back to his London shop and also wondered if his behavior might indicate guilt. She wondered what the inspector might make of his blunt statement.

She was standing there considering this when she heard someone coming down the stairway. She looked up to see that it was young Dr. Oliver Rush.

She said, "I thought you were at the hospital."

Looking rather embarrassed, he said, "I forgot about the funeral. At the last minute I decided to attend it. I hired a hackney cab but due to leaving late and the fog I didn't get here in time."

"You could have at least come out to the graveside," she said.

"I would have," he said, uneasily, "but when I arrived here Samantha came to me with the news that her father was having a violent spell. She begged me to go up and give him some sedation. Feeling this was more important than anything else that is what I did."

She said, "Then you surely can't be blamed. My husband is having a carriage made ready to take him to the hospital. If you hurry out to the stables I'm sure you'll catch him."

"Thank you," the young doctor said. "And please believe that I did want to attend the funeral."

"Of course I do, otherwise you'd not be here," she said. "Do go quickly or you'll miss your drive back!"

Dr. Rush made his way out and she went to the drawing room window in time to see him hail Terence's carriage just as it was headed out to the street. The carriage halted and the young doctor jumped up into it and then it drove away. Susan left the window with still some doubt in her mind about his story. Somehow it had not run entirely true.

A little later when she met Samantha on the landing she mentioned her meeting with the young doctor and that he'd claimed Samantha had enlisted his services to treat her father.

Samantha's gaunt face showed annoyance. "That is not true," she protested. "I happened to mention that my father was restless and he insisted on going up to check on him."

She was surprised. "Didn't he administer him a sedative at your request?"

"Certainly not at my request and surely without my knowledge," Samantha said indignantly. "He seemed anxious to go up to father as if he were trying to fill in the time. His version of the event is greatly exaggerated."

Susan was much disturbed by this account of the incident. It seemed to indicate that Dr. Rush had lied to her for some reason. And she could only speculate whether the reason might have something to do with Sally's murder. He had behaved oddly on this morning of the funeral. That is, if Samantha's version was correct, and sometimes the gaunt woman took the liberty of twisting facts to suit her own whims.

It was a puzzling and worrisome situation. And she was now worrying about dressing and getting away in time to have her meeting with Inspector Ragsdale at the Bull and Bear. She remained in her room until it was time to leave and then she quietly made her way downstairs thinking she might escape the house without anyone seeing her.

But her hopes were doomed. Just as she reached the bottom of the stairs an angry Angelica came down the hallway to greet her. The blond woman declared, "Do you know that Phillip has locked himself in the study?"

"He said he might."

"Why?"

Susan said, "He became very depressed after the funeral. He spoke of drinking himself into a state of forgetfulness."

"A miserable excuse!" the blond woman declared scornfully. "A drunkard's excuse! He is doing this deliberately to upset me!"

"I'm sorry," she said.

Angelica stood there in a seeming state of desperation. She twisted her hands feverishly. "There must be some way to get to him and stop this nonsense."

"I wouldn't worry too much," she told her. "After he's had enough to drink he'll likely come out. He's generally anxious for company when he's drinking."

Angelica glared at her. "And where do you think you are going?"

"I thought I might take a short stroll," she said. "My own nerves are not too good."

"Am I to be left alone with this awful situation?" the blonde demanded.

Susan saw that there might be trouble in getting away and this worried her. She said, "There's nothing to really worry about. Phillip has often gone on drinking sprees before. You have Samantha here."

"Samantha!" the attractive blonde said with icy disgust. "You know how much use she ever is to me!"

"I'm sorry," she said. "I'm dressed for a walk and I think I should go. I won't be long."

Angelica eyed her with cold suspicion. "You're so determined about it I declare you must be meeting someone. Are you and that young Dr. Rush having secret rendevous?"

She blushed. "You know that's not so. Dr. Rush just left in the carriage with Terence."

"I vow you have something in mind," Angelica said grimly.

"I have a walk in mind and I'm leaving now," she told her. And to spare any further argument she started on her way.

Not until she stepped out into the cold fog of the bleak day did she feel at all free. She hurried along the driveway until she reached the street and then walked briskly in the direction of the Bull and Bear. She had visions of an angry Angelica spying on her from the window. At least with the fog the blonde couldn't watch her for long.

Now all she could think of was her meeting with Inspector Ragsdale and what he might have to say to her. She was mostly worried that the burly police inspector was suspicious of Terence and would challenge her concerning his guilt. Surely Terence had been upset to see her talking to the police official.

As she put more distance behind her she gradually began to think less of Willowgate and more of what her reception would be like at the inn. She reached a portion of the street which had a series of small shops along it and finally looming out of the fog above her appeared the colorful swinging sign of the Bull and Bear.

A carriage had just pulled away from its entrance to rattle away into the thick fog and its two elderly, jolly occupants entered the inn. She kept on walking and next made out the figure of the inspector's assistant as he suddenly came out of one of the several entrances to the inn.

The assistant, a thin man, saw her and waited for her in the middle of the brick sidewalk. As she came up to him, he removed his hat and said, "Mrs. Ward?"

"Yes." She was nervous but saw that the assistant was a sly-looking man with a huge nose and a wart near the very end of it. "Is the inspector here?"

"He is," the assistant said. "He has taken the liberty of reserving one of the pub's private rooms on the second floor since your discussion will be of a personal nature. I will show you up there."

"Very well," she said, though she was getting more on edge every moment.

He led her up a flight of narrow stairs to a long corridor. She could smell the combined odors of ale and good roast beef up there. He came to a halt and opened a door for her on the left of the corridor and said, "You can go right in."

She did and discovered the burly Inspector Ragsdale seated at a table already enjoying a plate filled with roast beef and all the trimmings. A tankard of ale sat beside his plate. The big man rose and bowed to her.

"How do you do, Mrs. Ward. Accept my apologies for settling down to my meal before you arrived. But time is of the essence and I hoped I might finish before you got here." He paused and showed a grim smile on the broad face with the heavy gray side-whiskers. "And of course there was always the chance that you wouldn't appear."

"I said I would come and I am here," she told him quietly.

"A woman of your word. Something I admire. But then I have a special admiration for American women, Mrs. Ward. I visited your country several years ago on official business and I may say I was impressed with it and your people."

"Thank you," she said in a small voice.

"Won't you please be seated," he said, moving forward

and dragging out a chair for her. "And will you join me in some food? I'd be delighted and it will only take a moment to serve you."

"No, thank you," she said, sitting down. "But you go ahead and finish. I don't mind."

The burly man stood there hesitantly. "You're sure?"

"I am," she said. "In fact I'd feel guilty if I interrupted you in your meal."

"Ah, American women! I told you!" he said with admiration, and he sat down to the roast beef again. "This is very good of you to come here," he said.

"You told me you had something important to discuss with me," she said, watching him closely. The bald man finished with his plate and took a drink from the silver tankard of ale. Then he touched his napkin to his lips. He said, "I know a great deal about you and your marriage, Mrs. Ward."

She sensed the change in his manner. An almost cold note had come into his voice. Now he was completely the professional police officer. His sharp eyes were fixed on her.

She said, "Please go on."

"I know about the courtship in Boston and the wedding in Philadelphia," he said. "I even know about your stay in New York while waiting for a sailing and the frequent disappearances of your husband. Those disappearances which culminated in his vanishing the first night you spent at the Grand Hotel in London."

Susan was shocked at his offhand recounting of all these personal details of her marriage to Terence Ward. She said, "How have you learned all this?"

"We have our methods," he said without showing any expression. "I also know that your husband held back the information that his first wife had been murdered, presumably by Jack the Ripper, and that he had gone through a period of cocaine addiction. Do you think he was fair to you in withholding those things?"

She hesitated. "Not when you took at it so coldly. But he has offered good reasons for his silence in both instances and I'm inclined to accept them."

Inspector Ragsdale sat back in his chair and brushed his hand against one of his heavy gray side-whiskers. He said, "A doctor with a dubious record goes to America to escape notoriety and meets a lovely young heiress and by deceit woos and wins her. Correct?"

"No!" she protested, her cheeks flaming.

Inspector Ragsdale eyed her sadly. "Worst of all he wins her love. I'm very sorry about that, Mrs. Ward. I'm afraid the doctor has truly victimized you. And do you not know what the next logical event will be? Your murder, I'm certain. Not only will he inherit a tidy fortune to sustain his cocaine habit, but he will have removed a possible witness to his previous guilt from the scene. It is my theory that he already regrets marrying you for that reason."

"I can't believe any of it," she told him emotionally. "My husband is not that sort of man!"

The inspector sighed. "All right, let us deal in facts. All the Jack the Ripper murders have taken place while he has been in England. When he was away in America they ceased. On his return they started again. Several of them have been in his very district and one of the victims has been his wife. Now we have the case of a maid employed by him. All murders done by someone with extensive medical knowledge."

"That doesn't mean that my husband is guilty. There have been several doctors living at Willowgate. What about Dr. John Morley, who killed himself after Ruth Ward's murder?"

"Coincidence. He was a cocaine addict and unable to rehabilitate himself to the extent of your husband. Not that

I'm sure he is in the clear as he pretends to be."

"You've made up your mind!" she exclaimed. "You've decided that he is a murderer and Jack the Ripper!"

"He's our best suspect at the moment," the inspector said. "The night of Sally's murder he went to a dive not too far from where you live and obtained cocaine. We have sworn proof of that."

"He did it because he had an important operation the next morning and felt he needed the drug to give him a needed lift. It is part of his dependence on the drug which still remains. He confessed that to me!"

"I have a different idea," Inspector Ragsdale said sternly. "I think he took the cocaine and became temporarily the fiend known as Jack the Ripper, who has been guilty of so many bestial medical murders. I think he killed the maid, Sally, while on a high from the drug!"

"No!" she said brokenly.

"I believe your husband to be the most celebrated murderer in British history," the inspector went on evenly. "Everyone up to and including Queen Victoria has been writing the newspapers demanding that Jack the Ripper be brought to justice. And I think I can do that very thing by proving that he is your husband, Dr. Terence Ward!"

"You are wrong!"

"You think so?" There was sarcasm in his tone.

"I'm certain of it!"

He rose very deliberately and came from around the table. He said, "Very well. You have your opinion and I have mine. I'm going to ask you to back up your opinion with a risk to your life."

"Anything to prove Terence innocent."

"I can't guarantee it will do that," the inspector said. "I understand you have been threatened several times at

Willowgate by the ghost of Dr. Ward's first wife."

"Who told you that?"

"The young man who is living there, Dr. Oliver Rush."

"Are you so sure he is not mixed up in the murders?" she asked, remembering the young doctor's strangely confused excuse for coming back to the funeral and then missing it.

"I can vouch for that young man," Inspector Ragsdale said. "He has an uncle who is high in the ranks of Scotland Yard. It was no accident that Dr. Rush was placed in a position to work with your husband and live at Willowgate."

She gasped. "You mean he was sent there as a spy."

"I prefer to call him an intelligent observer. And he has done his work well, Mrs. Ward. So now I propose a plan whereby we can bring the murderer out in the open and at the same time end the appearances of the Willowgate ghost, for it is my opinion that your husband assumes the macabre disguise of a shrouded female when he sets out to murder. Our Jack the Ripper is a clever female impersonator, playing the phantom role of one of his victims."

"It's too fantastic!"

"I think not," he said calmly. "My plan involves you making a target of yourself for the phantom or Jack the Ripper or whatever you propose to call the murderer. Are you willing?"

"Yes."

"Very well," the inspector said. "Today you were a mourner by the graveside of Sally. Tonight I want you to take a lantern and go out to that cemetery alone. Make any excuse you like, say you have suddenly discovered the loss of a valuable cameo or some other piece of jewelry you were wearing. Or make no excuse at all, but go out there when you think all the house is at rest. It is my belief that Jack the Ripper lives at Willowgate, likely in the person of your husband, and that he will follow you out there and attempt to murder you. I will have men waiting to come to your rescue and we will have caught our man!"

"And if no one tries to attack me?" she asked.

"Then we will know our man is wary and have to try some other plan."

She got to her feet. "I'll do it," she said. "Just to prove to you that Terence is not Jack the Ripper or a murderer!"

Inspector Ragsdale changed his mood and became more kindly. He said, "For your sake, my dear lady, I trust that will turn out to be the case. But you must be ready to accept the other possibility and be brave. Let me add that Dr. Rush is a strong admirer of yours. You can count on him no matter what happens."

"Thank you," she said, in a small voice. "But I have full faith in my husband."

"I am amazed at your loyalty," the inspector confessed.

"Le us set a time for your excursion to the cemetery. Shall we say ten o'clock?"

"Very well," she said. "Ten tonight."

The inspector saw her to the sidewalk and she walked back alone in the fog. Her head was reeling with all that had been said in that private upper room smelling of beef and ale. She had not guessed that a time of revelation was so near. Now it seemed that she had placed herself in a position in which she would establish her husband's innocence or his guilt. She'd had to take up the challenge because she believed in Terence. But already small doubts were nagging her.

When she reached Willowgate it was midafternoon and the old house was still cloaked in a heavy gray mist. Inside she found that Phillip Ward had come out of the study and was sitting asleep in one of the drawing-room chairs with a huge medical book open on his lap. She went close to him to study it over his shoulder and saw that it was a volume on anatomy. The drunken man still lamented failing as a surgeon.

She went directly to her own bedroom and tried to prepare for the ordeal ahead. She decided to complain about the loss of a prized brooch at dinner and thus set the stage for her trip to the private cemetery. She did not see Samantha or Angelica until she and Terence went down to dinner. He had arrived home in good time and she was grateful for this. Never had he seemed more kindly or attentive.

When she told him, "I do believe I lost my mother's brooch at the graveside today," he seemed concerned.

"Are you certain?" he asked.

"I'm going to make another search after dinner," she said. "If it's nowhere in the apartment I have to have lost it outside. And the most likely place is the cemetery."

He gave her a wry smile. "You wouldn't think of going there looking for it tonight?"

"I don't know," she confessed. "It means so much to me I'd almost consider it."

"That would be both ridiculous and foolhardy," Terence said. "Let me know. I'll go take a look for you if you wish."

But she was careful not to mention it to him again and he seemed to forget about it. There was good reason for this since Phillip arrived at the dinner table ugly after his long day of drinking and he and Angelica staged an unpleasant scene at the table.

They went to bed around nine. She lay very still waiting for the sound of her husband's sleeping. He had to report at the hospital early in the morning and had professed a great weariness. Now he slept and she very quietly got up from their bed and dressed. Then she made her way out of the apartment and downstairs to a closet where she knew several lanterns were stored. She found a suitable one and lit it. Next she left the sleeping house by the front door.

The fog had not abated any, in fact it was thicker than it had been in the afternoon. As soon as she stepped outside, the lantern's glow was muted by the thick mist. All the fears she'd ever known since coming to Willowgate came to torture her. But she pushed on toward the cemetery filled with the determination to prove her husband's innocence.

But what if he were guilty? She knew that was remotely possible and she must be ready to face up to it. She also knew this plan of the inspector's might fail and then nothing would come of her terrifying challenge of the dark, foggy night.

She made her way through the dripping willow trees and on inside the gates of the private cemetery. Now the glow of the lantern caught the shadows of gravestones and the occasional tomb. She slowly made her way through the wet grass, fearful of every tiny sound and movement, her heart pounding with terror, and her whole being tense at the macabre atmosphere of the old graveyard on this fog-ridden night.

At last she reached the freshly filled grave of Sally. And for a moment she pictured the murdered girl's thin young face and her yellow pigtails. Surely it had been a cruel fiend who had murdered the girl, but not Terence. Her husband wasn't capable of any such crime.

She stood there not knowing what to do next. But she did not have long to question herself. All at once she heard a rustling from the bushes near the grave and then very slowly the shrouded phantom began to emerge. She saw the horror of Ruth's decayed and shrouded face, just as she'd experienced it before. Now the ghost plunged across the grave to attack her and as she staggered back screaming the glow of the lantern caught the glint of the surgical knife in the ghost's hand.

The shrouded phantom raised the knife to plunge it into Susan but it never found its mark. At the same instant

Inspector Ragsdale and his assistants sprang from their nearby hiding places and seized the surprised and struggling phantom. It was a brief struggle.

By the time Susan recovered herself the phantom was unmasked and standing silently a prisoner of two of the inspector's men. Susan gave a low cry of dismay as she saw the cold, grim face of Angelica.

The inspector came to Susan with the shroud and mask she'd used as a disguise in his hand. He said, "It seems your gamble paid off very well, Mrs. Ward. We have our killer and it isn't your husband."

It was then that Susan collapsed. When she came to she was in the bed in their own bedroom and a concerned Terence was seated on the bed beside her.

He said, "You almost sent me in a panic you've been so long coming around!"

Instant memory of that moment of horror in the graveyard returned to her. She raised herself on an elbow, "Angelica!" she cried.

He nodded. "Yes. I'm very much afraid that she is guilty of all the murders. That Jack the Ripper has turned out to be a woman."

"But how could she wield a scalpel as she did? Like a surgeon!"

Terence frowned. "You forget she had access to all Phillip's textbooks and his fine surgical instruments. He discovered she'd taken one the night of Sally's murder and began to suspect her. That is why he drank himself into a stupor the day of Sally's funeral. He already knew Angelica was a murderess but he didn't know what to do about it. As soon as the police captured her he quickly confessed all he knew."

Susan gazed at her husband with horror mirrored on her

pretty face. "Then she also murdered Ruth!"

"Yes. Put that down to jealousy."

"But why the others?"

"The curse of Cain," he said. "Like many other multiple murderers she discovered she enjoyed the thrill of matching her wits against the authorities. The thing became a game for her. I'm sure she also has to be a little mad."

As it turned out the authorities decided the same thing and Angelica Ward was sent to an insane asylum to be confined there for the balance of her life. Shortly after she was placed in the asylum she became violently insane and she died within a year. Her death came at about the same time the senile Dr. Simon Ward passed peacefully away in the attic apartment of Willowgate.

Phillip Ward no longer wished to remain in the house of bitter memories and so he moved to a small stone cottage in another part of London. Samantha went with him as his housekeeper. So the great mansion of Willowgate was left to Susan and Terence. They redecorated it and changed it from a house of brooding horror to one of happiness. Young Dr. Rush emigrated to America, vowing to find a girl like Susan.

Dr. Donald Farrow and his sister Agnes remained as friends and neighbors and Terence and Susan often visited the invalid woman. Inspector Ragsdale seemed to be haunted by the old mansion and on several occasions visited them at the house.

On his last visit he told them, "Was Angelica Ward truly Jack the Ripper as most of us assume? I'm not sure. I know she murdered Ruth and Sally, but when it comes to the others, many in Whitechapel, I sometimes wonder."

Susan told him, "But there have been no more Jack the Ripper murders since she was captured?"

"I realize that," the burly man said. "But I sometimes

worry that it proves nothing beyond the fact that the series of crimes happened to coincide. I have the uneasy feeling that maybe fifty years or a century from now information will be discovered to prove that there was another Jack the Ripper responsible for those other crimes."

Terence smiled wanly. "So you still hesitate to take the credit for capturing the Ripper?"

"I do," the inspector said frankly. "He may have just been wily enough to stop his killings with the capture of Angelica, safe in the knowledge that she'd be blamed for all the murders and there would be no further investigation. It wouldn't be unlike him. He was sly."

"You say him," Susan exclaimed. "So you must believe it!"

The inspector rose with a grim look on his broad face. "To tell you the truth I'm not certain at all. I doubt if I ever will be. But you two be wise and forget about it."

They saw the inspector to the door and because it was another night of gray mist watched him stroll out into the fog. When he'd vanished in the night they closed the door and went back to sit before the fireplace in the study.

Terence took her hand in his and said, "The inspector told us not to think about those bad times again."

"I know," she said. "But we will. We'll never forget. And perhaps I don't want to. Because through it all I never lost faith in you!"

"That makes it bearable," Terence agreed, "even worthwhile." And he drew her close for a kiss to their future happiness.

5/00